THE THIEF WHO PULLED ON TROUBLE'S BRAIDS

Amra Thetys: Book 1

MICHAEL McCLUNG

DEDICATION

Always and ever, for my crazy chickens.

CHAPTER 1

When Corbin showed up banging on my door at noon one sweltering summer day, I can't say I was particularly happy to see him. It should come as no surprise that one in my profession tends to sleep during daylight hours. And since I tell no one where I live, I was more than a little annoyed to see him.

"Hello, Amra," he said with that boyish smile that tended to get him past doors he wasn't supposed to get past. He stood nonchalantly at the top of the stairs, one hand on the splintered wooden railing. Well, what was left of the railing. Most of it had disintegrated before I moved in. He was looking ragged. Dark bags under his eyes, stubble that had gone beyond enticingly rough to slovenly. The yellow-green shadow of an old, ugly bruise peeked above his sweat-stained linen collar. His honey-colored locks were greasy and limp.

"Corbin. What the hells do you want?"

"To come in?" He kept smiling, but glanced over his shoulder.

"If you bring me trouble, I'll have your balls." But I cracked the door a bit wider, and he slipped past me into the entry hall.

"Take your boots off if you're going to stay, barbarian. You know how much that rug is worth?"

"Depends on who's buying, doesn't it?" He sat down on the bench in my tiny foyer and worked his laces loose. "Nice robe," he said with that silky voice of his, but I could tell his heart wasn't in it. I pulled my wrap tighter, and he chuckled.

"Don't worry, Amra. The knife sort of spoils the effect anyway."

I'd forgotten I was still holding a blade. I don't answer my door without one. Come to think of it, I don't do much of anything without one. I made it disappear and frowned at him.

"You can't stay here, and I'm not lending you any money."

He stretched, wiggled the toes of his stockinged feet. "Money I don't need. A place to stay, maybe, but your garret isn't what I had in mind." He looked at me, and I could tell he had something gnawing at him. This was no social call. "You have anything to drink? I'm parched."

"Yeah. Come into the parlor."

I'm not terribly feminine. I've a scarred face, a figure like a boy, and a mouth like a twenty-year sailor. In the circles that count, I'm recognized as good at what I do, and what I do is not traditionally a woman's profession. I was a few rungs up from pickpocket. Still, in the privacy of my own hovel I enjoy a few of the finer, more delicate things. Silks and velvets. Pastels. Glasswork. When Corbin walked into the parlor he gave a low whistle.

"Amra, this is positively decadent. I expected bare walls and second-hand furniture." He wandered around, peering at paintings, books, the tiny glass figurines I kept in a case.

"Shut up and sit down. You want wine?"

"Have anything else?"

"No."

"Then I'd die for some wine." He sprawled out on the huge Elamner cushion I used for seating. He stretched his legs and smiled. I shook my head, and went to dig around in my sorry excuse for a pantry. I came up with a couple of relatively clean glasses. When you live alone and don't entertain at all, ever, doing the dishes is a relatively low priority. I uncorked a palatable Fel-Radoth that was better than he deserved. But it was too early to punish myself with swill.

I poured a couple, handed him one and leaned against the wall. He took his and put it back in one gulp. I shuddered, snatched up the Fel-Radoth and corked it.

"What?" he said.

I put the bottle back in the pantry and came back out with a jug of Tambor's vile vintage. It was barely fit for cooking with. I dropped it in his lap. "Remind me never to give you anything worth drinking again."

He shrugged and began sipping straight from the jug.

"You don't want to borrow money. You don't want a place to stay. What *do* you want, Corbin?"

He sighed, reached into his voluminous shirt—I'd thought he'd looked a little lumpy—and brought out something smallish, wrapped in raw silk. About the size of my two fists put together. He held it out to me. "I need you to hold this for a while."

I didn't take it. "What is it?"

"Ill-gotten gains, what else? But I earned it, Amra, and a lot more besides. This is all I managed to come away with, though. For now."

I took it from his hands. Reluctantly. I was surprised at the weight. I knew without looking that it was gold. I unwrapped it, discovered I was right. It was a small statuette, one of the ugliest things I'd ever seen.

I held a bloated toad, two legs in the front and a tail in place of hoppers in the back. Pebbly skin. Two evil little emerald eyes, badly cut. It was devouring a tiny gold woman. She wasn't enjoying it. The artist must have been familiar with torment, though, because her small face was the very picture of it despite the crude overall rendering. All but her head and one arm were already in the belly of the beast. Her hand reached out in a disturbing parody of a wave. I don't think that was the effect the artist intended.

"Where did you get this ugly bastard?" I asked him.

"Doesn't matter. The place collapsed around my ears as I was leaving anyway." He leaned forward. "It was part of a commission, Amra. There were a dozen other pieces. I got them all, and it wasn't easy."

"Where are all the rest?" I asked.

He scowled. "The client double-crossed me. He's got the others, but he wants this one bad. Bad enough that I've got him by the balls." His face brightened and he chuckled. "I'm getting my original commission, plus a bad faith penalty. All told, it's three thousand gold marks, and I'll give you a hundred just to look after this thing for a few hours."

I frowned. I'd known Corbin for three years; he was a good thief and a good man. Thin as a blade, with one of those faces that sets girls blushing and whispering to each other behind cupped hands, and prompts women to cast long, speculative glances. He had the longest lashes I've ever seen on a man or a woman. He was an easy drunk, and so drank little, though he was free with rounds. He had fine-boned hands and honey-blond, wavy hair, and when I told him 'no' one night when his hands got too free, I didn't have to back it with a blade and I never had to tell him again. Maybe once or twice I wished I hadn't been so firm, but as regrets go, it was a mild, melancholy one. The 'what if' game isn't much fun to play.

That said, Corbin was not the smartest man I'd ever met. Not stupid; stupid thieves don't live long. But his cunning was situational. When it came to people, he seemed never to really understand what they were capable of. Or perhaps he just didn't want to believe what people were capable of was the rule rather than the exception.

"Amra? It's easy money."

"Too easy," I replied, taking a sip of wine.

"Gods above, woman! I thought you might want a little extra moil, and I need somebody I can trust. But if it's no—" He reached for the statuette, and I slapped his hand away.

"I didn't say no."

Corbin smiled, showing his remarkably straight, remarkably white teeth. It made me want to throw the ugly thing back in his face. But a hundred marks wasn't something I could walk away from. I should have, of course. Just as he should have cut his losses.

"One condition," I said. "Tell me who you're squeezing."

He didn't like that. The customer was supposed to remain anonymous. It's the closest thing to a rule there is in the business. He frowned.

"Oh, come on, Corbin. You said yourself they tried to screw you out of your fee."

"True. Why would you want to know, though?"

"Because if I'm going to stick my toe in the water, I want to know what's swimming around in it."

"And whether it has teeth. All right, fair enough. It's some Elamner by the name of Heirus. All I know is he's rich as sin. He's rented a villa down on the Jacos Road. It backs onto the cliffs. He's got hired blades all around him, and a hunchbacked little flunky named Bosch that does all the dirty work. Bosch is who I dealt with. I never met the Elamner himself."

I'd never heard either name. "Is this Bosch a local?"

"He's Lucernan, but not from the city I don't think. A Southerner by his accent."

"One more thing. Where did the statues come from?"

6

"I took them from an old, old temple in the Gol-Shen swamps. Like I said, the place doesn't exist anymore. I barely got out with all my limbs and digits. It wasn't the best time I've had." He took another swallow of Tambor's Best and corked the bottle.

"Any other questions?"

"For a hundred marks, I'll watch your back if you want. They tried to stiff you once; why wouldn't they try again?"

"The first time I got sloppy. I still can't figure out how they knew where I stashed the other pieces. I'd swear I wasn't tailed. I brought that one along to the meet, to show the goods. They were supposed to pay out then and I'd tell them where the statues were. When I got there nobody showed up and when I went back the rest of it was gone." He grinned that easy grin of his. "I guess I fouled up their plans a bit by bringing that one along instead of leaving it with the rest. It was just an impulse. A virtuous impulse that paid off. Like I said, I've got them by the balls this time."

I wasn't so sure of that.

"So now you're supposed to bring it and you won't. What's to stop them from trying to beat it out of you?"

"Don't worry about it. I've arranged a nice safe place to conduct business, and a long tour abroad after. For my health."

I grunted. I've been called a pessimist. And a suspicious bitch. And then there were those who weren't interested in compliments. But this wasn't my play, it was Corbin's. I'd back him to whatever extent he wanted me to. A hundred marks and friendship had earned that.

"Whatever you say, Corbin." I hefted the idol in my hand. "When will you come get this?"

He stood and stretched. "Midnight, or a little later."

"And if you don't show up?"

"If I'm not here by dawn, the statue's yours. Melt it down, though. Make sure there's no chance they get it on the open market." He went back to the hall and started lacing his boots.

"What about you?" I asked.

"What about me?"

"If you don't show up."

He shrugged. "Take care of Bone for me. You know where I live."

"I don't like dogs."

"No, you don't like being responsible for anyone but yourself. For the meltdown value of that thing, though, you can put up with Bone. Besides," he said, "he likes you. Oh, and Amra? This one is lovely." He held up a tiny blown-glass hummingbird he'd filched from my cabinet, stuck it in his pocket with an incorrigible smile. And with that he was out the door and clumping down the rickety steps.

I locked the door behind him. Nothing had better go wrong. Bone was a massive brute of a mongrel. Who slobbered. Copiously. I wasn't having that all over my house.

I took another look at the statuette. It was just as ghastly. The gold wasn't particularly pure, and the carving was crude. Ancient grime darkened the creases. There wasn't much polish to it, so I assumed it hadn't been handled very much or very often.

A half-dozen frog-aspected gods, godlings and demons came to mind, but none of them were less than four-legged, and only two were man eaters. I shrugged. It either belonged to some backwater cult nobody'd ever heard of, or it was something from before the Diaspora. If it was the first, it was worth nothing more than the meltdown value. If it was the latter, it could be worth much, much more. To the right person. Given Corbin's experience, I thought the latter was more likely, but I'd melt it down just the same if it came to that.

I put the ugly little statue in my hidey-hole and went back to sleep. I dreamed that I could hear its labored breathing there in the wall, punctuated by the shrieks of its meal. And when I woke just after sunset, it was with a miserable headache and a mouth that tasted like I'd been on a three-day drunk. What, you've never been on a three-day drunk? Take a big bite out of the next dead cat you see lying in the gutter; you'll get the idea.

CHAPTER 2

Feeling restless and out of sorts, and with a handful of hours before midnight, I washed and dressed and went out into the night. My headache was a nasty little needle spearing both temples.

Downstairs, I could hear the swirling and clacking of bone tiles from the gaming tables of the Korani Social Club. Endless rounds of push were played down there by gruff old men far from their island home. Once a month they had a dance, and the peculiar music of a three-piece hurdy-gurdy band moaned and shuddered and wheezed up through the floorboards. Otherwise they were good neighbors.

I walked a bit in lantern light through the Foreigners' Quarter, along streets that looked more dangerous than they really were. Lucernis had grown beyond all thought of being quartered long ago, but the name had stuck. I liked it there. It was close enough to the harbor to catch a breeze in summer, which in Lucernis was worth the rotting fish stench that came with it. And the Foreigners' Quarter was home to all stripes and classes.

I had the least trouble there of anywhere in Lucernis. But a woman walking alone still has to watch herself and her surroundings, and I regularly put up with a nominal amount of abuse and innuendo. I dress like a man and have the figure of a boy, and if someone gets close enough to see my face and figure out my gender, they're also close enough to see a few of my more prominent scars. It's usually enough. If not, I've spent a lot of time working up competence with knives.

I wandered down through the Night Market, past every imaginable type of hawker, and grabbed a meal from Atan. Atan is a burly Camlacher street vendor who smells of the charcoal stove he's habitually bent over, face red and shiny from the heat. He doesn't use any ingredients that are too foul or too rancid. He keeps the gristle quotient to a minimum. I've never gotten sick off it, though I'm never entirely certain what I'm eating.

"What kind of meat tonight, Atan?"

"Edible," he grunted, fanning the charcoal.

"Sounds like something my mother would have said."

His broad, craggy face grew even more morose than was usual. "Yes, compare me to a woman. Why not? I cook, I must not be a man." He shook his head.

I think all Camlachers must have a touch of the morose, as if they'd fallen from some great height and were bitter about having to slog down in the mud with the rest of humanity. Comes of being a defeated warrior race, I suppose. Grey-eyed Atan should have been handling a broadsword, not meat skewers

"Nothing wrong with being a woman," I told him. "But then I'm biased, I suppose."

"Yes. Next time I will wear skirts and use the powder for my face. Go away, you."

"Good night, Atan."

He waved me off. I ate abstractedly, walking down Mourndock Street, not really noticing the food. Slowly the headache faded.

I didn't really notice the old lady, either, until it became obvious she'd planted herself in my path. She was wearing a threadbare but clean dress, an embroidered bonnet perched on her iron-grey hair. She was even shorter than me. I tried to move around her, and she shifted to check my forward progress once again.

"My pardon," said the crone. "You seem troubled."

"Whatever you're selling," I replied, "I'm very much not in the market."

"You seem troubled," she said once more, and I noticed her piercing green eyes. Everything else about her shouted 'granny,' but those eyes said something different. Something closer to predator. I pulled back. "I'm fine, thanks."

"Oh no, I don't think so. I see a darkness in those pretty hazel eyes of yours. And I see shadows gathering behind you." Her hand shot out and grabbed my wrist.

"You'd best let go of me, Gran. I don't want to make a scene on the street. But I will."

She wasn't hearing me, wasn't really paying attention to me anymore. Those green eyes had suddenly turned a stormy grey. Bloodwitch. I was having a conversation on Mourndock Street with a bloodwitch. Bloody fantastic.

"I See blood, and gold," she said, her voice gone all hollow. "I Hear a mournful howl. Fire and Death are on your trail, girl, and behind them the Eightfold Bitch makes her way to your door. One of Her Blades has noticed you. But will it find your hand, or your heart? Unclear, uncertain...."

Twisting away from her, I broke contact. My hand itched to have a blade in it, but that would have been foolish. Bloodwitches are nasty enemies. "Kerf's balls, woman, what the hells are you talking about?"

She smiled, a little wanly. Her eyes were slowly losing their grey sheen.

"Oh, you have a world of trouble coming down on you, girl. Come see Mother Crimson when it gets bad. You'll find me in Loathewater." She moved to pat my hand, but I retreated. One more cryptic look and she was gone in the pedestrian traffic.

"Kerf's crooked staff," I muttered. "Aren't fortune tellers supposed to tell you how lucky you are?" But I knew my own words for what they were – bravado. I needed a drink. Bloody bloodwitches. I'd rather deal with mages any day, if I had to deal with magic at all. At least mages generally didn't bother with cryptic nonsense.

Of all those with powers—mages, bloodwitches, even daemonists—it was bloodwitches that bothered me the most. Mages could alter reality to suit their will, and daemonists gained power from the inhabitants of the eleven hells. But mages were few and far between, and I'd heard more than once that whatever power they drew on to work their magic was weakening. Daemonists, for their part, were hunted down wherever they were found, and for good reason. They all eventually tried to open a hell gate, it seemed, and the world had enough problems without hordes of demons, daemons and daemonettes wandering around it at will. Fortunately, opening hell gates took considerable time and effort, and the process was, apparently, not something you were likely to miss if you were anywhere near it.

Bloodwitches, though... They were strange, and their powers were disturbing.

Let's just say I disliked the idea of someone being able to turn all the blood in my veins to rust. Add to the fact that some of them could see the future, or make the dead speak, and you'll understand why they weren't often invited to parties.

I spent some time at Tambor's wine shop, at one of the outside tables, sipping vinegar from an earthenware cup and listening to gossip.

When Tambor's closed I was in a sour mood. I've never been good at waiting. I can do it, but I don't like it. I was worried about Corbin and more disturbed by what the bloodwitch had said than I cared to admit or think about. I had no idea who this Eightfold Bitch was or could possibly be, but I knew bloodwitches were the genuine article. I'd had the misfortune of seeing one at work in Kirabor, once. I'm really not squeamish, but seeing what she'd done to half a dozen men had left me tasting my dinner a second time.

With an effort, I filed it all away for later rumination. If there was trouble on the way, it would come whether I worried about it or not.

About an hour before midnight I made my way back home to wait for Corbin, feeling aimless and surly. And worried.

Midnight came and went. I read; my mother had taught me letters before she died, and Lucernis had some of the finest and most poorly guarded private libraries of any city I knew of. But then, who steals books? Besides me, I mean. If you can read, you're probably wealthy enough to buy your own.

It was one of those slightly racy romantic histories from the past century. Normally I'd have enjoyed it, but my mind wasn't on it. I kept reading the same passage over and over, and it kept slipping away from me. Finally, I tossed the book aside in disgust and settled for pacing.

Three hours after midnight my creeping suspicion had filled out into an atavistic certainty that Corbin had come to a bad end. But all I could do was wait out the night.

CHAPTER 3

Cock crowed while the sky was still black. I was out the door. Whatever had happened was probably long over and nothing I could do about it, but I couldn't just sit there. A heavy dread was slowly churning my guts. There were only two places to go. I decided to start with Corbin's house, and check at his mistress's if he wasn't there.

It was a long walk to his hovel off Silk Street, through streets mostly deserted. Few hacks worked at that hour, and fewer were likely to take me where I wanted to go. There was a baker's boy stumbling late to work, white apron trailing unnoticed on the filthy cobbles; I didn't have to be a seer to know he had a beating in his near future. There was a lamplighter on low stilts, snuffing white-yellow flame with his telescoping pole. There was the odd wagon creaking and rumbling its way towards Traitor's Gate Market, down cobbled streets. But mostly it was just blank dark windows and shuttered doorways, until I turned onto Silk Street proper.

Silk Street is where the boys and girls, and men and women in Lucernis practice the oldest profession. At that hour, there were far fewer wares on display, and those that were tended to be coarse stuff, made increasingly coarser as grey dawn seeped into the sky. Those left working were ones who had a quota to meet, a figure that had to be reached to avoid a beating or an eviction or the symptoms of one withdrawal or another. The ones who were willing to accept rough trade. One trollop in a soiled satin ball gown, his blue chin bristling out from under streaked face powder, cast aspersions on my manhood when I ignored his proposition. I would have found that amusing on several levels in other circumstances.

I had avoided their fate when I was younger. Bellarius, where I had grown up and almost died countless times, was not kind to its poor. I'd made theft my profession, and discovered quickly I was good at it. But it made me uncomfortable to see how I might easily have ended up. It always did. I deepened my scowl and ignored the various opening ploys, trudging past with my hands in my pockets.

As always, when the tired come-ons had no effect, they turned to jeers and catcalls. Anything to elicit a response. They faded behind me as I turned off Silk Street on to the nameless, barely-more-than-an alley where Corbin's hovel was. The entire street was lined with narrow wooden houses, two and three stories high. Some needed paint; most needed to be torn down. Almost all of them were built far too close together. A few of the houses were so close to each other you couldn't have walked between them sideways. It needed only a small fire and a stiff breeze to all go up.

As I got closer to Corbin's pit, I could hear howls, and a rough old voice screeching in anger.

"Shut it! Shut up, you mongrel! Shut it, Gorm take you!" The sound of something breakable being hurled against something less breakable. The howls went on and on, heart-breaking. I've heard wolves calling to each other across snow covered hills, mournful and lonely. This was nothing like that. This was grief made audible. Other dogs in the area had begun picking it up, and other voices, rough and querulous with interrupted sleep, yelled protest in several languages. A door slammed. I broke into a trot. For people like me, there are damned few coincidences. Expecting the worst helps to keep you from getting sucker-punched—and in my world, there are always fists waiting to hammer on the unwary.

I saw the old man first. The one who'd used Gorm's name in vain. Not that there's any other way to use it, Gorm being dead and all. The old man was a greasy grey smear of nightshirt and skinny, hairy legs with knobby knees. He was swinging something that would have been a truncheon if it was shorter, would have been a club if it was thicker. His back was to me; I couldn't see what he was beating. Then I came up on him and saw that it was Bone. The geezer was bringing his stick down on Bone's spade-shaped head, again and again. The dog kept howling, and refused to flinch. Behind Bone was something wet and lumpy.

The mind takes in images in little snatches, and sometimes they make no sense at first. It looked like the dog was guarding a pile of garbage. I saw the red, and knew it for blood, and knew from the quantity of it on the cobbles that someone had died badly. But these little pieces of knowledge didn't fit together right away. There was just the gut anger at an old man beating a dog.

I plucked the stick from his hand on a back swing and rolled it around across his windpipe. He squawked and gagged and clawed at the stick. I pulled him back a few steps, turned him around and planted a boot in his scrawny backside, letting the stick go with one hand. He sprawled to the cobbles, hacking. I guessed he'd stay down for a bit, so I went to check out the dog.

With his skull-thumping at least suspended, Bone had turned his attention to the bloody lump. He was nuzzling what I recognized as a hand. When it flopped back down to the street, I saw that the last three fingers were missing. Cut off cleanly, at the last joint. Of their own accord, my eyes travelled to the corpse's face.

It was Corbin. He lay huddled at an unnatural angle, maybe a half-dozen steps from his own doorstep. Bone started up that soul-splitting howl again. Shutters were opened here and there. Cautious heads popped out, saw blood, disappeared again as if by magic. I felt a numbness take hold. I turned back to the old man.

"You see a body in the street, and all you can think to do is beat the dog that disturbed your sleep?" I squeezed the stick so hard the tendons in my hand began to creak in protest. He gabbled something unintelligible and began to scramble away from me on his backside, looking like something between a lizard and a crab. His yellowed eyes were wide. Like all bullies, he was a coward at heart. I was surprised he'd worked up the nerve to beat Bone. The mutt was eighty pounds of brindle-covered muscle, with a face that was fashioned for malign animal intent.

I let him scuttle away into his ramshackle house across the street, and I let Bone keep howling. There was nothing to be done about either. As for Corbin, I didn't cry for him. Bone was doing enough of that for the both of us. I squatted down next to him, realized I was still holding the old man's courage stick. I threw it at his front door.

I figured I had at least a few minutes, and probably much longer, before what passed for the law in Lucernis made an appearance.

CHAPTER 4

Somebody gets cut up at night in Lucernis, maybe the corpse disappears before dawn, before awkward questions start getting asked. Nobody sees anything. Nobody wants to get involved. Not in a neighborhood like Corbin's. Not usually, anyway.

I took a good look at what they'd done to him. Maybe I had an idea I would like to reproduce it in reasonably accurate detail. Maybe I just wanted to know what I was up against. I don't know. But when I moved to look over the damage, Bone stood between me and Corbin.

"Too late now. Where were you when it happened?" I realized that was actually a good question. I put my hand out to him, murmured soothing nonsense. He sniffed. I suppose he recognized me, because a little of that murderous look went out of his eyes. But he wasn't letting me manhandle what was left of his master. I settled for gently rolling Corbin over on his back. Which earned me a rumbling growl.

The damage was extensive. Somebody had worked him over with a knife. It looked as if maybe some of it was controlled, precise. Like his missing fingers. The rest just looked like Corbin had tangled with somebody in a vicious barroom brawl. Slashes on his arms, his face. Rents in his shirt suggested he'd been stabbed maybe half a dozen times, two or three of which, depending on how deep they went, could have been immediate life-enders. I'd know more if I could undress him, but I didn't really need to know any more, and it wasn't worth struggling with the damn dog over. Maybe he was the wiser. It was done, and maybe all that was left was to mourn.

I stepped back from the body and looked around. The sky was perceptibly lightening. No crowd yet. They'd show up after the law did. I walked over to Corbin's house.

The flimsy door gaped. It had been busted open from the inside; that much I could tell. The lock was engaged; the frame had given way first. I supposed an eighty-pound dog could eventually have battered his way through, given sufficient motive. I glanced inside. Heavy furniture, a little dust. I hesitated. Whatever had happened, it hadn't happened in there. With the neighbors peering out behind curtains, I decided to leave it for the constables.

I ended up wishing I hadn't. The constables came around the corner as I was walking back to Bone. They knew where they were going, and they knew what to expect. Somebody had probably sent their kid down to the local watch station.

It was a pair. A fat, balding one and a young one so tall he looked stretched. Neither wore the entire uniform; Baldy had forgot or forgone his tabard, and Too-tall had substituted his deep blue woolen trousers for a paler, cooler, more wrinkled pair of linens.

Too-tall glanced at me, at the dog, at Corbin. He sighed. Baldy said, with a voice like gravel, "Can you shut that mutt up?"

"No."

He whipped out his cosh and laid it across Bone's head with a speed that belied all his fat. Bone went down in mid-howl. I took a step forward, fists tightening. I caught myself. Baldy pretended not to notice. He slipped the billy back through the leather thong at his belt and said, "So what happened here?"

"I don't know. I was passing by. I heard the howling. I saw a man beating on something, so I came up behind him and took his stick away. Then I saw the body. I stayed around until you showed up."

"Just a concerned citizen, eh?"

"That's right."

"You know the deceased?"

"No." While Baldy questioned me, Too-tall was going over Corbin's corpse. Checking pockets, checking wounds. I watched him from the corner of my eye.

"Let me see your hands."

I held them out, palms down. He took a good look at my nails. No blood. He swirled a fat finger; turn them over. I obliged. No blood in the creases. Baldy looked at me, clearly not believing a word I said. He probably would have worn the same face if I'd mentioned that water was wet.

"Any weapons?"

"Yes."

He put his hand out, and I gave him two of my more obvious knives. He gave me the eye that he probably used on husbands that beat their wives, kids that cut purses, day-laborers that thumped their bosses and made off with the strongbox. The one that said he knew I was holding out on him. I kept his gaze. Finally, he shrugged. "Why don't you go stand over there by the wall." It wasn't a suggestion. I went. He put my knives in his belt and turned to his partner.

"Arwin? Anything?"

"Well, he's dead, sure as shit. Somebody carved him up like a midwinter roast."

"Better let's move him out of the street."

They hauled Corbin over to the edge of the street, then Too-tall— Arwin—went back and dragged Bone over next to him. They had a muttered conversation, then Arwin went inside Corbin's house, and Baldy started knocking on doors, questioning neighbors. The geezer came out and started pointing his finger at me. He got in Baldy's face. Baldy took it for a while, then jabbed one fat finger right into the old man's sternum so hard he stumbled back, face ashen. Baldy said something, and the geezer retreated back inside his hovel, but I could see him twitch aside dusty curtains every so often.

I could have slipped off, easily enough. I think Baldy half-expected me to. I don't think he would have cared, especially. It was just another dirty little murder in a bad part of town. He didn't pin me for it. He was just suspicious on general principles. If it hadn't been for the damned dog, I would have taken off. But I could see his barrel chest rising and falling. And Corbin had paid me to keep it that way.

Then Arwin came out of Corbin's hovel, and by the look on his face I could tell things had changed somehow. He called his partner—Jarvis, apparently—and when Jarvis lumbered over, showed him something small enough to fit in one closed hand.

I heard Jarvis mutter "Isin's creamy tits," and then "better get the inspector." And I knew things were about to get much more complicated.

Jarvis made it plain that he now cared very much whether I disappeared, so I settled up against a garden wall that had been whitewashed sometime back in the reign of Orvo VII. Bone started to stir, and when Jarvis looked like he was going to beat him down again, I volunteered to take care of the dog. He shrugged. I hauled Bone up in both arms and carried him over to my spot, and kept a careful hand on his thick leather collar. Old boy was dazed. He kept licking his chops, and he'd developed a tremble. It wasn't that hard to keep him down.

We waited maybe half an hour. The sun rose higher, and the heat climbed. There was no shade. Arwin had gone off at a trot. Jarvis continued the door-to-door. A couple of night watch I could handle. An inspector would be much trickier. I was reasonably certain there weren't any little posters tacked to a wall in some constable's office featuring my face, but I didn't relish someone with brains and authority knowing what I looked like. Sometime down the road, one and one might be added to make two. But it was too late to do anything about it now. And I wanted to know what they'd found in Corbin's house.

The hansom pulled up about eight o'clock. There were no official seals on the doors. Arwin jumped out, folded down the two steps, and then a slight, middle-aged man stepped down. His hair was iron grey, cropped short and brushed forward over his long skull. He had a vaguely horsy face; prominent front teeth that his lips didn't quite cover. His eyes were mild and blue in a face that was very dark for a Lucernan. He was dressed soberly, in deep maroon velvets that were too heavy for the season. They were immaculate, but a bit threadbare. I could see where his white hose had been carefully darned. His shoes were black and polished, well-made but worn. The buckles were plain silver. He wore no jewellery.

His only concession to the climbing heat was a stiff collar undone. He glanced at me, and I knew he'd just filed away my face in the library of his mind, for future reference. He spent a minute or so with the body, then went inside Corbin's house. Jarvis followed him in, leaving Arwin outside.

They spent quite a while in there. By that time a crowd had begun to gather. Jarvis came out and spread a blanket over the body, then went back inside. Three more constables showed up, and Jarvis poked his head out to tell Arwin to go home and get some sleep. Arwin shrugged. He didn't leave.

Finally, one of the new constables stepped out, looked at me, crooked a finger. I dragged Bone along with me, heavy and uncooperative and dazed.

They'd done a thorough go-through. Not that there was much there to begin with. I am familiar with the careful search, having done it myself many times. It's nothing terribly destructive. Furniture shifted to spots no one would consciously place it. Rugs rolled up and put out of the way. Wall hangings taken down. Much like someone was preparing to move house. But of course, the purpose is to thump the walls, listening for hidden cavities, and check out all the undersides of tables and chairs and desks, the backs of mirrors and paintings, the mortar between stones, the joins between boards. I didn't give them good odds on finding Corbin's hidey-hole, wherever it was. He'd been too much of a professional.

The inspector was sitting at Corbin's kitchen table, going over some papers. He glanced up, took in me and Bone.

"Constable, see if you can find some water for that dog, would you?" He went back to reading.

Jarvis made a face. And did what he was told.

The inspector pointed to a chair, and I sat, still keeping hold of Bone's collar. Jarvis found a bowl and, after a second, an earthenware jug that sploshed. He put both down on the table in front of me, a little harder than was necessary. I sniffed. It was water.

"Thank you, constable." And after a second, "I'll call you if I need you." I poured while Jarvis trudged out of the kitchen. Bone wasn't interested. He sort of folded up at my feet, panting, eyes glazed.

The inspector finished the page he was reading and placed it face-down on the table. I doubt he believed I could read, but he'd noticed me glancing at the paper. Careful bastard. All I could tell from my momentary, upside-down vantage was that it was at least similar to Corbin's handwriting, and that it looked like a letter.

"My name is Kluge. Why don't we start with a few simple questions. What is your name?" He wasn't taking notes. I got the impression he didn't need to.

"Marfa Valence." There were probably ten thousand Valences in Lucernis, and a goodly portion were likely named Marfa.

"Occupation?"

"None."

"Place of residence?"

I gave him an address to one of the bolt-holes I kept the rent current on. Which of course was about to change.

"What was your relationship with the deceased?"

"No relationship."

He just kept looking at me with those mild blue eyes. I could see that his pupils were ringed with a thin band of azure. Pretty. He spoke first.

"I'm going to tell you a few things, Marfa, and then we're going to start again." He stuck out his thumb. "Judging by the wounds on the body, we are looking at two separate attacks. Three fingers were removed some hours before the fatal wounds were inflicted. That suggests torture, and I can think of too many scenarios that might fit to make this some random street slaying. If I had to guess, they tortured him, and then they let him run for a while. All the way to his house, within sight of safety. Then they finished him off, messily."

"Why would anybody do that?"

"Who knows why? Maybe for the sport of it." He sighed. I started to say something and he said in a quiet tone, "I'm not finished yet."

He held up an index finger. "The man out in the street is Corbin Hardin, known to some by the rather unfortunate moniker 'Night-Wind'; a thief with a penchant for stealing rare art of all types."

Middle finger. "Corbin Hardin was also known as Corbin Hardin det Thracen-Courune, second son of Count Orlin det Thracen-Courune. Father and son have been estranged for some half-dozen years."

He reached into a pocket and set a heavy gold signet ring down on the scarred table, one with a noble coat of arms on its flat, bevelled-edge top. I didn't try to hide the flicker of surprise that crossed my face.

Ring finger. "Corbin Hardin was a source of deep shame and embarrassment to his family while alive. But now that he's dead, that is most definitely about to change. I guarantee you, Marfa, the father will want blood. Gallons of it. And he'll get it."

Little finger. "I'm the poor sod who caught all of this in his lap, which is what I deserve, I suppose, for coming into work early. Your cooperation in this matter will ensure that any involvement you may have had will remain confidential. And you are involved, somehow. I don't think you did it. Tell me what you know, and I'll do my best to convince Count Orlin's people that you were just an innocent passer-by."

He smiled wearily. "Now, let's start again. Your name is Marfa, you've no occupation, you live at Borlick's rooming house on East

Southcross. Now tell me again what your relationship was with the deceased?"

~ ~ ~

He was good at what he did. I didn't try to get too tricky. I gave him an abbreviated version of the truth. Corbin had stopped by, told me he had business that might get ugly. Told me he'd been away in Gol-Shen on a commission. That the customer had tried to stiff him. Asked me to look after his dog if he hadn't turned up by dawn. No, I didn't know what the commission was. No, I didn't know who the customer was, where they were meeting, why anyone might want to kill him.

I tried very hard to make him think I was telling him the whole truth, by telling him part of it in great detail. I described the shape Corbin was in when he came to see me. I told him what we drank, tried to remember word for word some of the things he'd said. I did my best to seem both reluctant to be telling the law anything, and eager that once I'd said my piece, I'd be forgotten. And of course I didn't say anything that might implicate me in anything. I gave the slight impression that Corbin and I had a now and again relationship of an intimate nature.

I kept the statuette out of it, and any mention of the Elamner Heirus and his flunky Bosch. I wanted them for myself. If the constabulary went barging in, the bastard would disappear if he hadn't already. And so would the other statuettes. I didn't think he was going anywhere, though. Not without the toad. Not if he was willing to kill for it.

Maybe Kluge thought I was holding out, maybe not. His face was unreadable. He presented an air of weary competence, an honest man doing his best in a job that didn't pay enough. He was going to do a kindness to someone caught on the periphery of something ugly.

Right.

I had no doubt he'd toss me straight into Havelock prison if he thought it would get him farther along. A dirty little street knifing had turned into the death of a noble, albeit a disgraced one, and people with enough clout to bury Kluge in an unmarked grave—literally—were going to be second guessing his every move soon enough. He was going to cast me back, just to see where I might lead him. I was going to have to look over my shoulder every damn where I went.

When he finally waved me away with the admonishment to make sure I was available for further questioning, he'd managed to give me sweaty palms. He got up and walked me to the door, hand politely at my back. When he stuck out a hand to shake, I took it.

As soon as his hand touched mine, the little hairs on the back of my neck stood up and a chill ran down my spine. I walked outside, pretending I hadn't noticed a thing. I swore silently.

The son of a bitch had just used magic on me. Odds were he didn't need to detail men to tail me. He'd know exactly where I was, wherever I went. I hoped that was all he'd done. I tried not to think about all the nasty little things it was possible to do with just a handshake.

Corbin's body had been removed while I was inside, and the blood mostly washed away. The smell still lingered, though, and Bone set up a half-hearted howl. I collected my knives from Jarvis, who no doubt was hoping I'd forget them. Fat chance of that. They were perfectly weighted for me, and had cost me dear.

The damned dog didn't stop his howling until we were blocks away. I dragged him along by his collar. I was going to have to get some rope. He was giving me another headache. "Kerf's withered testicles," I spat, shocking a sweet-faced granny passing by.

Heirus the Elamner was going to have to wait. Hells, I couldn't even risk going back home until I'd done something about Kluge's leave-taking present. It had become necessary to get some magic of my own.

I set off for the charnel grounds. It was time to see Holgren.

CHAPTER 5

Holgren Angrado lived way the hells and gone on the other side of the River Ose, on the edge of the charnel grounds. And of course I had to walk it. No hack was going to pick me up while I was dragging eighty pounds of scarred, slobbering dog along. It was a two hour walk from Silk Street up to Daughter's Bridge, on what had to be the hottest day of the year. By the time we got there the rest of the morning had fled, and my temper was vile. At least Bone had stopped howling.

Lucernans are much like anyone else, except when it comes to death. I was born in Bellarius, myself, so I don't really understand their odd fixation with forms and observances and their peculiar ideas about the afterlife, but it seems to work for them.

There is only one true graveyard in Lucernis: The City of the Dead. It's a huge necropolis that butts up against the south bank of the Ose. Its gargantuan hexagonal wall is ten man-heights of alabaster stretching on and on. People visit, send letters to the dearly departed, have midsummer feasts there. Like any city, it has its rich districts and its poor. And like any city, if you don't pay your rent, you get the boot. Thus, the charnel grounds.

Those whose families would not or could not pay the annual mortuary tax were disinterred, and their bodies dumped with a distinct lack of ceremony in the city's charnel grounds. Which, I understand, is a bit like being taken from a civilized limbo and being cast into one of the less pleasant pits in the eleven hells. I could almost believe it, given the smell. Myself, I think dead is dead, and whatever happens to your body makes no nevermind, but like I said, I'm not from here.

Holgren was the only mage I knew well enough not to run screaming from. Why he chose to live next door to a field full of bodies in various states of rot I'll never understand. But I never asked him. I was afraid he might tell me.

I dragged Bone along dusty roads and past the occasional shack that was all there was of Lucernis northwest of the Ose. Holgren's house was low and long and dark, roofed in grey slate. It looked like it was poised to tumble in on itself. I made my way to the front door of his hovel, past the broken statuary and dead grass that made up his front garden, and banged the ancient brass knocker. And waited. And waited.

I was about to knock again when the door creaked open, revealing only gloom. There was no one on the other side.

"Holgren?" I called. "It's Amra." No answer. I shrugged, and Bone and I crossed the threshold.

My eyes adjusted. It was like any other sitting room, I suppose. More or less. A couch, dusty and torn. Delicate little tables covered with yellowing lace doilies. A porcelain teapot decorated with buttercups and morning glories. Dried flowers in a chipped vase. Threadbare rug. Less usual were the skulls and anatomical charts, the framed map of the eleven hells, the withered, claw-like Glory Hand casting feeble blue light from under a bell jar, the jars of preserved things that had no business twitching and sloshing in the corner of my eye. And the room was far cooler than it had any right to be.

I liked Holgren. I even trusted him, to a degree. But he was still a mage, and being around a mage was like being around a 'tame' lion. You could never fully let down your guard. They were just too powerful, and too unpredictable. Their motivations were too obscure. Ultimately, I think, the kind of power a mage dealt with on a daily basis pushed him, eventually, beyond mundane considerations such as right and wrong. He tended to think more along the lines of 'possible' and 'impossible', and the 'impossible' list was a lot shorter for a mage than it was for you or me.

Holgren had never been anything but polite and accommodating towards me. But there was always a first time. And considering how powerful he was, that first time would also almost certainly be the last time.

"Holgren?"

"Be with you in a moment," came a muffled reply from behind a door marked with sigils that writhed and twisted when I looked at them. I shuddered and took a seat on the couch. Bone put his rock-like skull in my lap. Almost instantly my pants were soaked in slobber. I sighed, and scratched behind his scored ears. There was a lump where Jarvis had bashed him, but other than that, he seemed fine.

A short time later the creepy door opened and Holgren sauntered into the parlor. He must have startled Bone, because the bruiser whipped around with a rolling, rumbling growl in his throat. Holgren stopped where he was, and his hawk-like eyes locked with Bone's. They stood like that for maybe half a dozen heartbeats, and then Bone shut up and dipped his head and his tail.

"You've acquired a loyal friend since we last met, Amra. Would you like some tea?"

"No thanks." I patted Bone. "Inherited, more like."

Holgren cocked an eyebrow. He was a tall, almost gangly man, with predatory eyes, a sharp nose, a generous mouth. His black hair was shoulder length and bound up in a ponytail. He was wearing black. He always wore black. Not much for fashion, this one.

"Listen," I said, "I might have brought some trouble to your door. I ran into a mage. He tagged me with some sort of spell."

Holgren pulled up a chair that had seen better centuries. Touched the teapot. The smell of chamomile suddenly wafted. He poured himself a cup.

"So tell me about it," he said.

~ ~ ~

I told him about Corbin, his commission, the favor he'd asked of me. I told him about Corbin's death and Inspector Kluge. He asked a few questions, but not many. He knew how to be circumspect, and didn't ask the questions that he knew I would be reluctant to answer.

Holgren lived on the same shadowy side of the law as me. He took commissions. That's how I'd met him. He'd subcontracted one of them to me, on the advice of Daruvner, our mutual fixer. He was a good mage, but I was a much better thief. Our skills actually complemented each other quite well, and we'd done three jobs together in quick succession. Then he'd stopped taking contracts. I found out later from Daruvner that Holgren

Angrado worked only when he had to. He'd make a pile of coin, then go into semi-retirement until it ran out.

Holgren sat, legs crossed and hand to lips, digesting what I'd told him. He shook his head. "Corbin told you he'd set up the meet in a safe place. Any idea where?"

"Not really. Obviously someplace not as safe as he thought."

"He could have been betrayed."

I shrugged. Probably. There was just no telling.

"This Kluge, what did he look like?"

I described him. Holgren shook his head.

"I don't know him. I don't know what sort of power he wields. I might assume that, since he takes a civil servant's pay, he is not terribly talented, but I don't like to assume." He tapped his full lower lip with one long forefinger. He was staring at me, through me. Long enough that I started getting the creeps. "Well," he finally said, shaking himself. "Nothing for it but to see what we can see. Come sit here." He vacated the chair.

I took a deep breath, then shifted from the couch to the chair. He stood behind me, which made me more than a little nervous. He put his fine-boned hands on my shoulders. He smelled of lavender, and under that, something acrid. As though he'd been working with chemicals. He didn't smell bad, just strange. Bone looked on from where he was stretched out next to the couch, a thin rope of drool slowly stretching to the floor from his black lips. I felt a little laugh bubble up at that, but choked it down.

The hairs on the back of my neck stirred faintly. Holgren shifted his hands to the sides of my neck, then cool fingers touched corners of my jaw, then my temples. My skin tingled and I repressed a shudder. It's not that it was unpleasant. It wasn't. It's just that it was... intimate. More intimate than I was comfortable with. And the feel of his magic had a different quality to it than Kluge's. More confident, somehow. More knowledgeable. Self-assured. The difference between a grope and a caress. I found myself blushing, and was glad Holgren couldn't see my face.

"You can sense me," he remarked, a faint note of surprise in his voice. I nodded slightly, and the feel of whatever he was doing changed, somehow. Became more business-like. More formal. Almost remote. I found myself at once relieved and vaguely disappointed.

Finally, he took his hands away. He sprawled out on the couch, and one hand dropped down. He rubbed between Bone's eyes with a casual knuckle, and the dog stretched out and presented his chest. Holgren scratched dutifully.

"Well?"

"Well, you were right. This Kluge marked you with a location spell. A basic working, really, but sometimes the basic ones are the most reliable. At some point during your conversation he must have collected something particular to you. Most likely a hair. Then he made physical contact with you, a simple handshake being quite sufficient."

I remembered his hand on my back, in all probability plucking a fallen hair. "That sneaky—and then?"

"And then he most probably winds that hair around something, perhaps a pin, and places the pin on a specially prepared map."

I frowned. "And then he watches the pin shift along the map as I go hither and yon."

"That's about the size of it."

"So what do I do?"

"Nothing. Right now, that pin is rolling around like a sailor four hours into shore leave. He'll know you've gone to see a mage, of course, but he would have known that if I'd simply severed the connection. Better he wonders who you might know who could tie his spell in knots."

"What? Why? You're putting yourself in line for unnecessary scrutiny, aren't you?"

He smiled. "When you came here you assured a knock on my door from the inspector, I think. I'd rather he come wary and respectful. When mages meet, there is a tendency towards discovering who has the greater talent. Occupational hazard, I suppose. Sometimes making the discovery can be hard on the furniture. Now he knows that, whoever I am, I am most likely his master in the Art. It will help head off any possible unpleasantness."

"If you say so. Still, I'm sorry to have gotten you involved. I owe you."

He waved it away. "I am sorry about your friend. And interested in these statuettes, to tell you the truth. If you care to, you can come by again and I'll take a look at the one you have. If it is pre–Diaspora, I might be interested in purchasing it from you. I'd give you more than a hundred marks for it, and it will never see the open market."

"I'll think about it. I have a feeling it might be useful to me in the near future." As a lure, or a threat. "I'll stop by tomorrow if I can."

"What will you do next?"

"Get some sleep. Find out what there is to know about this Elamner that Corbin contracted with. Decide how best to approach him." How to get in, knife him, and get out with a whole hide.

"What about this one?"

"Bone? I don't know. I've got a lot to do, and looking after that slob will be a pain." I looked at the dog. He'd fallen asleep on his back under Holgren's scratching, scarred ears splayed out like little wings, tongue lolling.

"You could leave him here, for now. Until you make other arrangements. I could use the company. And he will make a nice pretence for your visit here when the inspector comes calling."

I glanced around at the various bits of bodies under glass. "You aren't in need of dog parts, are you?"

His expression was one of pained indignation.

"Hey, I was going to make you an offer. Cheap."

~ ~ ~

I managed to catch a hack just south of Daughter's Bridge. On the ride back, I mulled over my options, tried to figure out what my next move was. Corbin's death had stirred up a hornet's nest.

Kluge and company would be scrambling to find someone to pin his death on, before Corbin's family came to town with blood on their mind. Heirus, I could safely assume, would still be looking for what he'd been willing to kill for. And of course some cold-eyed killers would be arriving in the next few days, come to collect their pound of flesh for Corbin's old man. From every perspective, all roads could at some point lead to me. It was too late for me to back out, even if I wanted to. I didn't want to.

There would be interesting days ahead.

CHAPTER 6

By the time I got home it was late afternoon. I was dead tired. Sleep beckoned. I checked my hidey-hole just to make sure the golden toad was still there. It hadn't hopped off. The heat was oppressive. I stripped down to my undershirt, grabbed a bottle of sweet white Gosland wine, and crawled into bed. I lay there sweating and thinking and sipping until sleep came.

Sometimes theft can be as simple and direct as a fist in an unsuspecting face, and sometimes it can be as complex as a military operation. And just like a bar-room brawl or a pitched battle, whatever plan you went in with, simple or complex, was bound to be stretched and twisted as events played out. But you'd better have some kind of plan, or you were going to get trounced. Or worse. I was planning a death, not a burglary, but in many ways that just made it easier. Taking a life was, in my experience, a damned sight less complicated than taking jewels from a hidden strongbox.

What I was facing was getting messier by the moment, however. I needed more information. I needed to act, rather than react. There was too much I just didn't know. Information had to be my priority. Without it, I'd end up stumbling into a knife. Or a noose.

So I needed to case Heirus' villa. And I needed to brace Locquewood, Corbin's fixer. I needed to find out more about that damned toad, and I needed to throw the various dogs off their various scents and give myself some breathing room.

One last swig and I re-corked the bottle and blew out the candle.

~ ~ ~

I slept far later than I usually do, deep into the night. But it was a restless, broken sleep, between the heat and the bad dreams. In my dreams I saw Corbin hacked up there in the street, except he kept grinning at me, white teeth pinked with blood. And there was the whispering. Like he was trying to tell me things. Awful things. Terrible truths it was better not to know. Things that made my head pound and my chest constrict.

And so, when an unfamiliar sound intruded, it woke me. Head throbbing, I cocked an ear to the dark. It came again; the stealthy creak of a shutter being slowly eased open. It came from the parlor.

Amateur. Should have brought some grease along, I thought, and slipped out of bed, knives in both hands. Every room in my house has easily accessible knives. I'd had a lover for a short time that found it off-putting. He went. The knives stayed.

It was near pitch black. The dark didn't bother me; I knew the layout of my own house very well and so the dark was more asset than liability. Sliding down the narrow hallway that connected my bedroom to the parlor, I kept low, presenting as small a silhouette as possible.

I caught him—it—as it was climbing through the window; a black outline against the faint glow from the moonlit street. A humanoid form; head, arms, legs, all in the expected places. But the head sported knobs and spikes in silhouette, and wicked looking barbs sprouted from the fingers, a dirty parody of brass knuckles.

Just seeing the outline of the thing made me want to kill it. Hate boiled out of my soul, an unreasoning, vicious hate tinged with disgust. I wanted to kill it. I had to kill it. I felt my lips pull back over my teeth, felt a snarl start way down in my lungs. I threw a knife. I aimed for the throat, but it shifted at the last instant, and the blade struck the meat of the thing's shoulder with a wet *thwock*. It hissed in pain and surprise, and toppled backward into the street. I rushed to the window, ready to cast again. It was too quick. I caught the barest glimpse of a mottled grey form loping down the alley. It was swallowed up by the dark an instant later, along with the unreasoning hate that had consumed me.

"Kerf's crooked staff," I breathed. And that was it. The whole thing, from waking to stabbing, had lasted less than a minute.

31

Now that it was over I began to tremble. I locked the shutter, went to the pantry and tossed down a large portion of the Fel Radoth that I'd banned Corbin from for gulping.

What in the eleven hells *was* the thing? I had no idea. What did it want? How had it found me? No idea. But I was certain it hadn't been some sort of mistake, no random break-in. I don't believe in chance. I believe in cause and effect.

As for the tide of hate that had washed over me, I had no explanation. But all of it was bound up together. Somehow. The fact that something could *compel* me to feel hate, or any emotion for that matter, made me feel a hot kind of hate toward whatever the cause was. Yes, I am aware of the irony.

The only cause I could think of was that damned golden toad.

~ ~ ~

I spent the rest of the night in a state of controlled panic, starting at every creak, every sound from the street. That thing had not been human, and it disturbed me more than I liked to admit that something could take control of my emotions.

I thought about how it could have tracked me. No way that thing had shadowed me all across the city, from Corbin's to Holgren's to my house. Not in that form, at least. But for all I knew it could be a shape changer. Still, I doubted I'd been tailed. Which brought to mind how Corbin had said he'd gotten careless himself, when he'd lost the other twelve statuettes. Something was going on, something I didn't understand. Maybe magical. Probably magical. I supposed it was possible that someone or something was looking for the statues with a different kind of sight. Hells, the creature could have sniffed the statue out for all I knew. In any case, I had to assume that the creature, presumably acting in Heirus' interests, had a way to find the statue wherever it was. Which made things more complicated than I liked.

When grey dawn crept through the shutters, I went down and looked over the alley the creature had disappeared down.

I found my knife halfway between streets. The blade was covered in a grey-green slime, and pitted with corrosion. I tapped it against a wall, and the tempered steel blade broke like chalk.

Shit. Good blades didn't come cheap.

~ ~ ~

My first stop of the day was Corbin's fixer. Locquewood had a small curio shop near the Dragon Gate. Most of his custom was from the manses along the Promenade, wealthy merchants and minor nobility who could afford the expensive baubles he sold. I would have preferred to brace him after I'd checked out the Elamner's villa, but with last night's visitor, I was feeling pressed for time. Things were starting to heat up.

I came in the back way, through the service entrance. Bollund, Locquewood's muscle, sat whittling in the back room among packing crates and scattered straw. He glanced up when I came in, then fixed his attention back on his carving. I think it was supposed to be a pheckla, but mostly it looked like a turd.

"Bollund! Still twice the woman I am, I see. I need to talk to your boss."

Bollund glanced up at me, fingered the smashed gristle of what presumably had once been his nose. He'd been a bare-knuckle fighter before becoming ensconced in Locquewood's back room.

"You don't see 'im. 'E sees you."

"Well he needs to see me. Now."

Bollund smirked. He was two heads taller and his bulk could make three of me. He wasn't impressed and he wasn't intimidated.

I pulled out the toad from my leather satchel, unwrapped its silk covering. The buttery glow of the gold drew his beady eye.

"He's got five minutes, then I'm taking this to Daruvner."

Bollund's jaw clenched. He shifted his bulk up from the slat-back chair that somehow supported him. Locquewood was a fixer, not a fence, but Bollund knew enough not to make decisions for his employer where money was involved. The toad would fit in tolerably with the kinds of things Locquewood stocked his shop with. A little older, a little uglier, a little less precious, by appearances.

"Stay 'ere. Don't touch nothing."

"Yes ma'am."

He glared at me, then disappeared through an inner doorway.

I had no interest in selling the thing, of course. Not yet, and not to

Locquewood in any case. I just wanted to pump him for information. Whether I would get anything was doubtful; Locquewood's lips were tighter than a frog's arse, which was why he was trusted enough by untrustworthy sorts to be a fixer. But he might let something slip.

Locquewood appeared a few minutes later, a cadaverous dandy in pale yellow silk and bleached lace. He ran manicured fingers through thinning hair and licked his lips.

"Amra, you know the arrangement. You can't just show up—"

"I can do whatever I like when a man trusted to fix commissions gets one of my friends killed."

"What are you talking about?"

"Corbin. I'm talking about Corbin, Locquewood. The client you fixed him up with cut off a few of his more important fingers and then knifed him to death."

His pale face turned a delicate shade of green. "Why I never— that's—I don't know what you're talking about."

So Locquewood had been the fixer Corbin had used for this commission. I was fairly sure before, now I was certain of it.

"Save it. Corbin was a friend. He was killed because of this." I let him have a glimpse of the toad. If Heirus already knew I had it, I risked nothing. And Locquewood needed to know I wasn't just spouting off. "He died because of some damned statue, and because his fixer didn't check the client out well enough. That is, if you weren't in on it to begin with."

"Amra, I can assure you I, ah, am as circumspect as possible in all my business dealings. And I would never poison my own well, so to speak. I am sorry about Corbin's death. But I had nothing to do with it."

"Says you."

He got a little impatient. "What do you suspect me of? Having Corbin killed? Taking out a contract on him? Next you'll be accusing me of hiring Red Hand himself to do the deed."

"Who was the job for, Locquewood?"

"I'm sorry, I can't help you."

"Can't, or won't?"

"Both."

I could tell he wasn't going to give me anything more. That was fine. I'd planted the idea that I didn't yet know who Corbin's customer was and, hopefully, had set Locquewood on a collision course with Heirus the

Elamner. Locquewood had more than two marks to rub together; I was willing to bet he would spend what it took to send a message, and keep his reputation as an honest fixer secure. How much good it would do, I didn't know. But I figured stirring up trouble would help keep eyes off me. It's easier to swim unnoticed in muddy water, so to speak. Not that I know how to swim.

I glared at him, mouth tight. He returned my gaze with a bland one of his own.

"If I find out you had anything to do with this," I hissed, "you'll regret it." And I stormed out of his back room, slamming the door.

When I walked away from his shop, it was with a spring in my step. It had been a good performance. Maybe not good enough for the Clarion Theatre, but good enough. I was certain Locquewood had bought it.

My next stop was one I enjoyed less.

CHAPTER 7

The May Queen's Dream was a red brick, three-story building on Third Wall Road, with red painted shutters and riotous flowers in every window box. It was as far from the whores' cribs on Silk Street as silk is from a sow's ear, but it was a whorehouse none the less.

A frock-coated butler offered to take my satchel. I declined, and stepped from the staid entry hall with its dark wood panelling into the lush, cool parlor.

It had been a long time since I'd been here. I'd forgotten Estra's uncanny decorating tastes. It was a huge room, but managed to convey a sense of intimacy. A creamy marble floor glowed under crystal chandeliers lit at all hours, and the walls were covered in red satin. Plush couches and chairs were arranged around the room in such a way as to create little pockets that invited conversation and intimacy. There were fine sculptures and fine paintings everywhere you looked. A bar ran the length of one wall, dark stained oak topped with pink granite. In one corner stood one of the new harpsichords, though no one was playing it at the moment. And at the end, a grand, carpeted stairway led to the rooms above. The entire effect was somehow one of understated ostentation.

This was where Corbin had spent a fair amount of time. He came for the woman I was here to see, but also, I think, for the atmosphere. Perhaps it reminded him of the beauty he must have grown up with. Perhaps Estra had, too. They fought like rats in a bag, to hear him tell it, but he always went back to her. Their relationship wasn't placid, but it was... constant.

Only three girls lounged in the parlor. It wasn't even noon yet. A black haired, green eyed-beauty stood and glided her way towards me. Her pale skin was flawless. Her crimson lips were flawless. The cleavage that pushed out over the top of her whalebone corset was ample, and flawless. I struggled not to hate her.

"Good morning," she said. "Welcome to the Dream. Can I offer you some refreshment?"

"I'm here to see Estra. I have some news for her."

"Madame usually breaks her fast now. Shall I say who is calling?"

"Amra Thetys."

"And this is in relation to?"

"Corbin. Tell her it's about Corbin."

Something flickered in those emerald eyes. Those perfect lips gave the slightest twitch, as if they wanted to say or ask something, but knew better. Curious. She did a perfect little curtsey and glided off. I walked over to the bar and asked the elderly, white-coated barman for an ale. It was the cheapest thing they served. At the Dream, everything they served was quality, and none of it at bargain prices. But I wasn't looking forward to telling Corbin's lover he was dead. I needed something.

A few minutes later, Raven-hair, face remotely serene, ushered me into the ground floor apartments of the owner of the Dream, Estra Haig. The same taste that had furnished the Dream's parlor had turned a more intimate, cozy eye on the private rooms. Everything was sunlight and creams and pale pastels, crystal and blonde wood and greenery. Pleasing textures.

She was sitting at a small table in a beige silk dressing gown, the remains of her breakfast laid before her. She was a well-preserved, striking woman in her late forties. The morning sunlight that streamed in from the glass window showed high cheekbones and delicate crow's feet, long nose, strong jaw, and the loosening skin of her neck in equal measure. I wouldn't look that good at her age. Hells, I didn't look that good at my age. Even without all the scars, I wouldn't look that good.

She turned her grey eyes to me and smiled. We knew each other, slightly. Not enough to be chummy. If I was here with news about Corbin, I could read in her face, it wasn't anything she'd be pleased to hear. She had the look of someone bracing for bad news.

"Amra. Sit. Have you eaten?"

"I'm fine, thanks." I sat. "How are you, Estra?"

"Well, thank you."

"Listen. I'm sorry to be the one to tell you this. Corbin's dead."

She went rigid for a moment, and that haughty, aging, beautiful face went taut and still as a mask. She closed her eyes briefly.

"How. Tell me how."

I told her. About the commission, and about the Elamner. About the toad. She asked to see it, and I showed her.

"So this is what he died for," she said, and looked at it a long time before handing it back.

She asked the kinds of questions that nobody really wants to hear the true answers to. How did he die. Was it quick.

I didn't varnish it. I told her what Kluge had told me and what I saw. She asked if Corbin's fixer had anything to do with it, and I told her I doubted it. Then the questions dried up, and she just sat there, hands in her lap, staring off into nothing. She didn't cry. This one wouldn't cry.

"There's something else. Corbin was some sort of nobility. The black sheep, I guess."

"I know."

"Then you can guess that there will be heat coming down from the family. Heads are going to roll, Estra. Watch yourself, all right?"

"I have friends who will see it as their duty to shield me from any unpleasantness. But thank you for your concern."

We sat there for a little while longer, in a silence that was uncomfortable for me. I don't think she even noticed I was still there until I rose to go.

"What are you going to do now?" she asked.

"Me? I'm going to make the Elamner pay."

Her eyes grew hard. "See that you do. If you need anything, come to me. Just... see that you do."

I nodded. "Give me a little time before you start looking for other, uh, alternatives, all right?"

She smiled, without a trace of mirth. "You take as long as you need, Amra. Corbin was fond of you. He trusted you. I see that the feeling was mutual. Take the time you need to do it right. But if you cannot do it for one reason or another, tell me. So that I can make arrangements. Are we agreed?"

"Yeah. That's fair."

"What will you do with that horrid statue?"

"I'm not sure yet. Melt it down, maybe. Maybe sell it. Maybe drop it in the Ose."

She nodded, face expressionless. "If you need to... dispose of it, Amra, I would be willing to take care of it for you. It's the least I can do."

"Thanks. I'll let you know if I do."

I made my way out. There were worse people to have in your corner than Estra Haig. She wielded a sort of influence in Lucernis. Her contacts spanned all classes, from brute killers to Privy Court judges to noblemen to the heads of some of the merchant families. Hells, for all I knew, she might be on a first name basis with Lord Morno himself.

I took one last glance back at her. Still the aging beauty, but something had gone out of her over the course of a few minutes' conversation. She sat as rigid as ever, but one manicured hand was white-knuckled, throttling a silk napkin.

CHAPTER 8

It remained for me to find a safe place to stow the idol. I wasn't going to be taking it along on my reconnaissance of Heirus's villa, and I damn sure wasn't leaving it at home. I could think of no better place than at Holgren's.

I stopped by a butcher's, and bought scrap and bones for Bone. He was still my responsibility, and I didn't want to press Holgren's generous impulses too far. Then I found a hack willing to take me as far as Daughter's Bridge, and walked the rest of the way.

When I knocked, Bone's deep, thumping bark started up. This time Holgren answered the door himself, with Bone trying to butt past his legs. Holgren wore a sheepish grin. I suspected they had been rough-housing. Bone grinned and drooled and thumped his tail against the doorsill. I patted his head. It was like patting fur-covered rock.

"Hello, Amra. What have you got there?"

"Treats for the beast." I passed him the packet from the butcher. "And I brought that thing we talked about yesterday."

"Excellent. Come in, come in. It's a hot day. Would you like wine?"

"That would be nice." I entered and sat down on the dusty sofa.

"Inspector Kluge came around this morning."

"How did that go?"

"Oh, fine. He was asking after someone named Marfa. I told him she was my sister, come to give me a dog. Some chitchat followed, a few questions about Corbin. I couldn't help him, and he left it at that." He passed me a glass. It was a crisp Kirabor. Not cheap.

"Sorry to bring the law to your door, Holgren."

He waved it away. "I'm glad you brought him. The dog, that is."

"So you and Bone are getting along all right?"

"I'd forgotten how enjoyable it can be to have a companion. I haven't had a dog since... for a long time."

"Well I'm glad you two have hit it off. Though I could have used him around last night."

"Oh?"

I told him about my visitor, and the effect it had had on my emotions. He shook his head.

"I've no idea what it was, I'm afraid. I've never heard of anything that fits the description. Grohl are humanoid, and a rather ghastly grey color, but they bleed red like you and I, and don't have any protrusions around the head or hands. And they wouldn't come within fifty miles of a human habitation for any reason other than to burn it to the ground."

"Whatever it was, I'm pretty sure it was after this." I unwrapped the toad and passed it to him. "I think my burglar can track that statue, somehow. I don't have any proof. I just can't think of any other reason it would be trying to sneak through my window."

"There's no telling, really. You could very well be right." He held it, and a strange look passed over his face. He set it down on the table and wiped his hand on his vest in an unconscious gesture.

"There's something more to this than meets the eye, Amra. Something distasteful. Something dangerous, I think." He looked up at me. "Have you noticed anything? Anything unusual?"

"Other than monsters crawling through my window? No. It's unusually ugly, but other than that, no. Not really."

"No strange urges? No odd thoughts crossing your mind? No sudden sickness?"

"No, nothing like that. Except—"

"Except?"

"Nothing, really. Just bad dreams and headaches the past couple of days. When I sleep. I keep hearing whispers, and breathing. I think it's just the heat."

"Maybe so, maybe no." He frowned and stared at the idol for a time. "There is something about it. Something old. Ancient. And unclean. It looks post-Diaspora, but feels far older...." He trailed off. His mind was somewhere else. He began mumbling to himself, in no language I recognized. I sat quietly, sipping my wine. One of the privileges of being a mage, I suppose, is that you can be as strange as you like, and nobody dares comment. Finally he shook himself and took a deep breath. He smiled a small smile at me.

"Would you mind terribly leaving it with me? I'd like to probe this mystery a bit further. It's very odd, almost as if—well, anyway, would you mind?"

"Not at all. You'd be doing me a favor. Another favor, actually. Just watch yourself. Apparently, it's worth killing for."

He smiled an unpleasant smile. "I've ample protection, believe me. Anyone able to defeat my wards will have earned whatever they can take from me. Give me a few days, Amra, and I'll see what I can see."

I spent a few minutes being licked to death by Bone, then took my leave. Holgren waved, already distracted by the lump of gold on the table and, presumably, the old evil it represented.

~ ~ ~

Finding the villa Heirus had rented wasn't terribly difficult. I hired a hack and told him I wanted to take a leisurely afternoon ride. I put a gold mark in his horny hand and pointed him down the Jacos Road. He was happy to oblige, with a week's wages in his fist.

Walking would have been better, but there was a much higher chance of me being noticed. There isn't much traffic that far down the Jacos, and anyone walking down and then back would have been noticed by a relatively alert guard.

There were dozens of villas along the Jacos Road, ranging from weekend cottages and love nests to full-fledged farm concerns. But only three backed onto the cliffs. They were all relatively small, and crowded in on each other. It's not a huge cliff. The villas were built for the view.

The first, I happened to know, belonged to Gran Ophir, a shipping magnate. The second turned out to be deserted, and had been for years, by the look of it. Which left only the southernmost.

It looked innocuous enough at first glance. Ivy-covered brick walls about twice my height. A wrought iron gate, all curlicues and blunt spikes.

Glimpses of a two-story structure screened behind lush vegetation. But the ivy was actually adder-tongue, a thorny, semi-poisonous climbing vine, and if you looked close enough you could see the occasional tell-tale glint of broken glass mortared into the top of the wall. And beyond the whimsy gate, two visible guards, armed with sword and crossbow.

I let the hack go on about a mile further, until we came to a quaint little country tavern. I had a drink in their beer garden and watched golden bees do their thing in the late afternoon sunshine. I let my mind wander.

I had seen what there was to see, and knew better by now than to try and force any sort of plan. It would all fall into place soon enough. Theft is as much art as it is craft. Reconnaissance work was a big part of that art, that craft. The villa's security, from what I had seen, was professional. I'd circumvented worse. But I hadn't seen anything but the surface.

I realized I was about to break one of my own rules. I was going to rush a job.

Usually I took at least a week to plan a break-in. I liked to observe the comings and goings, scheduled and otherwise, familiarize myself with faces and body language and study the peculiarities of the layout. To see what doors were used, and when, and by who. Which windows were opened, and which were never opened. To see if a guard had a tendency to nod, or drink, or even scratch his arse. I like to get to a place where I can grasp the rhythm of a household intuitively. The smallest thing can give you an insight which can lead to a plan. But there was no place to loiter and observe along the Jacos Road, and I had monsters trying to crawl through my window in the middle of the night, and I was willing to bet that the only way to make sure that kind of thing stopped was to kill the mysterious Elamner behind those villa walls.

When I reckoned an hour or so had passed, I woke my coachman up from where he snoozed in the shade of an old oak, and we headed back to the city. I didn't so much as glance at the villa as we passed the second time. You take what care you can.

Once back in the city, I rented a horse from Alain the carriage maker. I wasn't about to walk back to the villa.

Alain wasn't really in the practice of renting mounts, which was one of the reasons I preferred to rent from him. Another was that I'd done him a good turn once, and he felt some obligation over it. I could almost trust him. He would do right by me and wouldn't get curious as to what I might be doing.

He had a very large work yard out in the Spindles, on the city end of the Jacos Road, and half a dozen carpenters in his employ. He was an honest, stubborn, self-made man who was doing very well thanks to his skill and his wife Myra's business acumen.

I walked through the gate into his yard, and was immediately confronted with a gigantic wheeled... *thing*. Like a carriage big enough for a giant to lie down in.

"Amra! What do you think of it?" Alain called from across the yard.

"I think I pity the horse," I replied. "What the hells is it?"

"They're calling it an omnibus. Fits forty passengers."

"I have no idea what you're talking about."

He punched me in the arm. "I'm talking about making money, woman. This here omnibus will troll the length of Orange Road all day every day. People will jump on, pay their two coppers, ride as far as they want. Transport for the working man!"

"As long as the working man works along Orange Road." Which, admittedly, thousands did. It was a very long, wide road. "Does Myra approve?"

He smiled. "She approves of the fee for building it, which I'll be collecting now that it's nearly finished. She's more cautious about the investment side of things. But you're not here to talk about omnibuses. Or is it omnibi?"

"You're asking the wrong person. And I do need something. A horse for the night."

Alain picked out a grey gelding for me. From the looks of him, the horse had an appointment with the knackers in the not-too-distant future. My trust began to diminish.

"He looks ready to collapse," I told Alain.

Alain scratched his ample stomach. "He's a gentle one, is Kram. And you sit a horse like you've a stick shoved up an uncomfortable place, Amra."

I glared at him, but he was right. I can keep a saddle. Just. Growing up very poor in a city built on the side of a mountain, I didn't get much opportunity to learn. Bellarius wasn't known for its horsemanship.

Alain promised to have the horse saddled and ready an hour after sunset, and I flipped him a silver mark. Then I went home to start laying out my gear.

A funny thing happened along the way. There was a boy—well, I say boy, but he was in his late teens. He was staring at me.

He stood in the shade of the column that supports the aqueduct above Tar Street, just on the edge of the Spindles, and he had the biggest, kindest eyes I'd ever seen. He also had a shaved head, and was dressed in the simple rust-colored wrap of an ascetic. He was staring at me, and smiling a little. I scowled and his smile grew.

He didn't try to approach me. I couldn't puzzle it out, so I stopped trying. Lucernis is full of all sorts. I went on my way, but could feel his gaze on me until I turned the corner.

CHAPTER 9

I hid Kram in a copse of pin oak and hackberry about a mile from the villa, tying the lead to a low branch. I don't know why I bothered. Kram was one horse utterly uninterested in wandering. He had the look of a convict who'd given up all hope of escape, and was just waiting for death.

I didn't expect to enter Heirus's villa that night; all I planned to do was take a good long look at the layout of the grounds, and see what sort of security measures he had in place. And I was going to do it from the relative safety of the deserted villa next door to his. That was the plan, anyway.

The night was dark, but not as dark as I might have wished. Here on the outskirts of the city, manmade light was scarce. No street lamps, no lanterns or candles from windows close on either side of the street. There were just the stars and the moon. But the moon was almost full, and cast a bright silver light down through a cloudless sky. I have excellent night vision; that advantage would be whittled down.

I spent the next half-hour scuttling through the weed-choked ditch that ran alongside the Jacos Road, moving as quickly and quietly as I could toward the villa. It was dry as a bone, which was a blessing, but I startled the occasional creature. An opossum, a snake. A couple other things I didn't get a good look at. I am a city dweller, and had been almost all my life. I distrusted nature. It was an uncomfortable, nerve-rasping journey.

I wore a dark gray cotton tunic and trousers, and a pair of black, thin-soled boots. In one pocket I had a black silk vizard, for when it came time to cover my face. Otherwise it was a distraction. Any article of clothing you don't wear on a daily basis can be distracting, and in my line of business, distraction can be fatal.

On my back was a pack chock full of various implements and instruments of the trade, all carefully stowed so as not to shift or make noise. It was far more than I usually took to a job, but I planned to make the deserted villa next to Heirus's my base, so I wouldn't have to lug everything around the entire time. My blades were lamp-blacked, so as not to cast a stray glint at an inopportune moment. I was as prepared as I could be.

The deserted villa was nowhere near as well-put-together as Heirus's. It had a wall, but it was low and made of wood and dilapidated, sagging badly in some spots. It had been hardly more than decorative when it was new. Now, honeysuckle and morning glory and creeping laver were slowly tearing it down. When I finally reached it, I crept along the side opposite Heirus's until I found a gap wide enough to squirm through. I did, dragging my pack after me. Once inside the grounds, I crouched, and listened for a hundred heartbeats. Nothing but the occasional call of a night gull, and the whisper of a breeze in the riotous growth that had once been a smallish formal garden. I watched the darkened, paint-peeling house for any sign of movement. Nothing. In the strong moonlight, the villa looked diseased.

And just as I had decided it truly was deserted, I heard feet crunching on a gravel path somewhere off to my left. I froze, knife in hand. I couldn't see anything; the foliage was too thick. I listened to whoever it was cross from my extreme left to almost level with my position, then heard the footsteps recede.

If I had to guess, it was a sentry, making a circuit of the yard. But I didn't have to guess. I had all night. I pushed forward, slowly and silently through the dense shrubbery until I had a clear view of the villa. It was a two-story affair. I could tell by the layout there was an interior courtyard. There were very few windows on the outside, all of them too small to fit through. All the focus would be in, toward the courtyard, which would likely be tiled, with a fountain in the center. Hallways on both floors would run along the outer walls. The question was, did the builder break from the traditional villa layout to take in the sea view from the cliffs? I couldn't tell from where I was, but thought it probable.

If the grounds were being patrolled here, they were undoubtedly being patrolled by Heirus's men. Whoever was in charge of his security was no idiot. Anyone interested in gaining access to the Elamner's villa would almost certainly make use of the abandoned dwelling next door. Gran Ophir, the deserted villa's northern neighbor, wouldn't bother with such security measures. His villa was for the use of a mistress who happened to be travelling. The interesting tidbits you pick up, sitting around Tambor's.

I had a decision to make. I had planned to set up shop in the unused building and observe the Elamner's grounds from the roof. See how many guards, and what sort of rotation. Whether there were dogs. See what I could see of the interior of the villa, from a safe distance. The patrol here had complicated matters. I thought about it, and decided the risks did not outweigh the possible benefits.

I sat there in the darkness, utterly still. Two tiger moths fluttered around my head, landed on my arm. Began to copulate. I resolved to ignore them, though they were as big as my palm. Distractions can be fatal. About a half-hour later the guard made another circuit. He was armed with short sword and crossbow. The sword was sheathed, the crossbow's stock tucked into the crook of his arm. He was professional enough. He scanned his surroundings and didn't talk to himself or hum or whistle. He wore a doublet and loose, almost baggy trousers tucked into low boots. He wasn't wearing chain armor, that much I could tell. I couldn't tell from this distance if his doublet was just padded, or if iron plates had been sewn into it. Either was common.

As he moved off, away from me and in the direction of Heirus's villa, I moved quickly and quietly to my left, toward the cliffs. There was my best chance of entering the dilapidated building.

Once I got to the back of the villa it was a case of good news, bad news. The good news was that practically the entire back wall was open to the air, a series of huge windows with dilapidated shutters, to afford a view of the sea. Most of those shutters were stacked haphazardly on the ground about twenty feet away. Now it was a series of open, gaping entrances. The bad news was that there was absolutely no cover from the house to the cliff other than that low, wide stack of shutters. And there were two more guards stationed just inside the building.

I eased back into the deeper shadow of a huge hackberry, and waited some more. Listened to the dull roar of waves crashing against rocks forty feet below. Eventually the roaming guard came around the far corner and exchanged a few words with his two companions. I couldn't hear what they said over the surf. One appeared to grunt and took over the walking duties, crossbow slung over his shoulder.

I decided gaining entry to the abandoned villa wasn't worth the risk. Once you get in, you have to get out. Again I was at a crossroads. Go home, think of some other approach. Or go ahead, into Heirus's villa, practically blind. I wasn't kidding myself. If I went into that villa tonight, it would be to kill the man. I could let this go, if I wanted to. Corbin hadn't asked me to avenge his death. All he'd asked me to do was look after his dog.

Kluge's words came back to me. First they'd hacked off his fingers, then they'd let him run. Then they'd killed him, just for the sport of it.

Tonight was as good a night as any, and better for being sooner rather than later.

I trailed the roving guard at a safe distance back toward my entry point, then made my way carefully toward the Elamner's villa through the dense undergrowth that had been the front garden. I reached the sagging wall and took a look.

Between the two walls lay about ten yards of open ground that ran all the way to the cliffs. Someone kept the vegetation trimmed there; nothing grew more than ankle high. I couldn't see anyone on the wall across the open space, but I would have bet gold someone was set to watch that open space. I could see a small wooden door set into the side wall of the Elamner's villa, and about ten feet from my position, a gap in the wooden wall of the abandoned one. Where the guards passed back and forth, no doubt. Where the watcher would be stationed. No doubt the roaming guard would give the 'all's well' every time he passed.

All right, time to take a little risk.

I made my way carefully, quietly along the sagging vine-covered wall that ran parallel to the Elamner's villa, back towards the cliffs. When I reached the corner of the old house, I vaulted the low wall, to keep it between me and the watchmen stationed in the abandoned villa. Then I crawled through the shadow at the foot of the wall the rest of the way to the cliffs.

I stopped and pulled the bag of resin out of my pack, anointed both hands, and stowed it away. Took a few deep breaths. Then, offering up a brief prayer to Vosto, the god of fools and drunks, I lowered myself feet-first down the cliff face.

I descended far enough that I would be invisible to anyone not standing directly at the cliff's edge. The cliff was granite, and offered good hand and footholds. But my pack put my center of balance too far out over the water, and the rock was slick. I did not look down. If I fell, I was dead. The fall itself probably wouldn't kill me, unless I hit one of the jagged rocks down there. But there were things in the water that would finish the job. Phecklas. Grey urdu. They don't call it the Dragonsea for nothing. And anyway, I can't swim.

Slowly, carefully, blinking away the sudden sweat in my eyes, I crabbed sidewise across the cliff. I keep myself fit; I have to. But in five minutes my inner thighs were trembling and the muscles of my upper arms burned with the effort. The surf pounded and growled, an empty stomach waiting for a morsel to fall on the teeth of the rocks below.

When I judged I had gone far enough, I slowly, carefully rose up and looked. I'd gone about three feet past the corner. Here, thankfully, there was no thorny, poisonous adder tongue to contend with. There was about two feet of rocky ground between the cliff's edge and the wall, and it was in deep shadow. It wouldn't get any better. I dragged myself up and lay on my stomach, panting. I thought I had kept myself in shape, but obviously I'd been drinking too much wine and not exercising enough. When I'd got my breath back I carefully wriggled out of the pack straps and dug out all I thought I'd need. It wasn't much, really. The small grapnel with the silk cord. Lock picks. Small flask of oil. Resin bag. A pair of heavy gloves to deal with the glass atop the wall. Weapons were already secreted on my person, more than I should ever have to use in one night.

Some thieves prefer to carry tools varied and complex. I've always preferred to travel light, unless I know I'm not going to be disturbed, or there is a need to bring something along for a specific task. This was reconnaissance work, and maybe blood work, not theft. I'd kill the Elamner if I could, but I didn't count on getting that lucky. There was just no telling what my chances were until I was inside. I slipped the vizard over my face and took up the grapnel.

The trickiest part about grapnel work is the noise. Steel on stone is a distinctive sound, in the dead of night. Which is why I wrap mine in cotton cloth. The tines will bite through the cloth if you've got a good catch, and if you don't, then you won't have to worry about steel dragging along stone when you pull it back for another cast. Not that I had to worry about any of that with the surf pounding. A bat would have been hard-pressed to hear anything.

I put my back against the wall and, silk cord coiled in one hand, lobbed the three-pronged grapnel up and over. It cleared the top of the wall, and I started reeling in line. It caught, and I tugged harder, finally putting all my weight into it. It held. First cast lucky. I worried about the glass sawing into the line. Nothing I could do about it.

The gloves were so thick they were a hindrance, but I went up the rope quickly enough, and after scanning the gloom inside for any movement, carefully and quietly cleared a wide space of the inset glass shards. Then I lay on the top of the wall on my stomach, and turned the grapnel around and dropped the line into the villa grounds.

There was a chance that the line would be noticed, but there was a greater chance that I would need a quick exit when it was time to leave, and having to recast the grapnel while people were trying to kill me wasn't something I wanted to do. You figure the odds and you take your chances. I straddled the wall, slid myself down, hung by my fingertips for a moment, and dropped down quietly into the shadows at the base of the wall.

I made my way as quietly as I could over to a darkened, shuttered window. I used a knife to slip the latch on the shutter, and then I probed gently beyond with its tip. No glass, no parchment window. Just a shuttered casement, starting at waist height.

I listened, took a peek in the crack between the shutters. Darkness and silence on the other side; a stillness that betokened an empty, lifeless room. I threw the dice and decided to slip into the room.

Opening the shutters a bare necessary amount still flooded the room with moonlight. I froze.

I was almost right about the room. It was lifeless, but it wasn't quite empty.

Sprawled on the floor with a dagger in his heart was the corpse of a man. Judging by his raw silk robes, his dark skin and his oiled, ringleted hair, he was an Elamner. Someone had chalked a protective circle around him on the parquetry. There was no blood. There was, however, a crazy grin on the corpse's face. A palpable sense of unwelcome poured out of that room, a... malevolence. As if the very air inside it wished me ill. Bad, bad magic that I'd probably be stupid to test.

Another tiger moth fluttered past my shoulder into the room, and instantly fell to the floor, lifeless.

Shit.

Something struck me then, once, twice, with blinding speed. I felt a flare of agony in my shoulder and cruel blow to the side of my head, and as I dove down into the black pit of unconsciousness, I felt once more the bile of unreasoning hate boiling up in the back of my throat.

CHAPTER 10

I don't know how long I was out. Not very long. The moon hadn't moved across the sky perceptibly. I sat up, trembling and dazed. My shoulder was on fire. I was amazed to be alive. What had hit me?

The creature that had tried to break into my place. That insane, all-consuming instant hatred was not something I was likely to forget, or mistake.

I've no idea why it didn't kill me. I would certainly have killed *it*, given the chance. With the feeling that welled up in me when it was near, I would have crawled through fire to slit its throat.

I shrugged. Now was not the time to be gathering wool. I did a once-over on myself and discovered a knot on the side of my head and a bloody shoulder.

And a missing dagger. I searched all around me in the dark beneath the window, thinking I had dropped it. It was gone. I shrugged, and sighed. Another knife lost to the creature, I assumed.

"All right," I breathed, "that's enough for one night, Amra." I closed the shutter and made my way back to the wall.

Climbing the wall was agony. I tossed the pack into the sea. There was nothing in it I couldn't replace, and I wasn't going to try and negotiate the cliff face with it. After a moment, I threw the sweat-soaked vizard after the pack. At this point, if somebody saw my face I was dead anyway.

Even without the extra burden, that twenty feet of cliff would have been torture. I doubted very much that I'd be able to go back the way I came. If I tried, I'd end up in the Dragonsea, and the scent of fresh blood would make sure I wouldn't last long. So I flattened myself down on the ground and crawled along the edge of the cliff, waiting for a crossbow bolt to find my back. I knew where it would hit. Just between the shoulder blades. A spot there the size of a gold mark burned and itched, waiting for the bolt to punch through.

When I finally made it into the slice of shadow cast by the wooden fence of the other villa, I retched, as quietly as I could. Nerves. The sour taste of bile filled my mouth again, and I quietly spat it out. At least I was breathing.

Making my way across the overgrown garden was payment for all my sins. I hadn't realized I'd committed so many. I took it slowly, everything in me just wanting to get somewhere safe, to stop moving, to still the waves of pain from my shoulder and head. At one point I started trembling uncontrollably and I was forced to lay there until it subsided, praying the roving guard wouldn't be attracted by the sound of the rattling brush.

Eventually I made it to the ditch. About halfway to the copse where I'd hidden Kram, I passed out again. I must have lain there for a long time, because when I came to, my clothes were damp with dew. I looked up at the sky. A couple of hours before dawn. I had to hurry. I pushed myself hard, and made it into the copse and to the waiting horse. He looked at me with liquid eyes that seemed to say that all life was suffering.

"Shove it," I whispered, and untied him and climbed into the saddle.

The ride back was its own brand of suffering. Every plodding footfall sent a jolt of pain through shoulder and head.

By the time I got back to Alain's, grey-fingered dawn was creeping up on the horizon. I half-fell off the horse and banged on the gate to the work yard attached to his house. After a few moments I could hear the bar being lifted, and then Alain's son Owin poked his head out. He looked at me and his mouth gaped.

"What, you've never seen blood before?"

"No. I mean yes, but not that much. Not on anybody alive."

"Are you gonna let me in?"

He opened the gate and I led Kram into the yard. Owin was exaggerating, but my shirt was ruined. If I went back out into the increasing morning traffic I would be noticed. I hate to be noticed.

"I'm going to need a change of clothes, Owin. Is there anything around that will fit?" Alain's entire family was large. I am not.

"Uh. I'll ask Mum. Just let me get Kram into the stable. Maybe you should sit down?"

"I might not get back up."

He took the horse into the narrow stable on one side of the yard, and then led me to the kitchen door of the house. I could smell bacon frying. I realized I was ravenous.

Myra, Alain's wife, was a huge woman. She had one of those handsome faces that seemed almost incongruous compared with her bulk. Huge wide eyes and perfect brows and full lips. Lustrous brown hair. She took one look at me and pulled the pan off the fire.

"What in Isin's name happened to you?"

I shrugged, which wasn't a great idea.

"Sit down. Looks like your shoulder's been torn to ribbons. And that smell! We'll have to burn those clothes. Strip out of that shirt."

Normally I would have bristled at anyone ordering me about. Not with Myra. As soon tell the rain to stop falling. Myra was Myra, an unstoppable force.

Five knives went onto the table. Myra made no comment. I had a hard time getting the tunic and undershirt off by myself. Caked blood glued them to the wound, and my abused muscles shrieked pain in protest when I raised my arms over my head. Tried to raise them. Myra helped, clucking her tongue and muttering all the while. She glanced at her son, still standing at the kitchen door.

"Owin, don't you have something to do? Whatever it is, it's not in here."

He blinked and blushed. "Ah. Yes." And he disappeared, ruddy cheeks and all. For all that he was only a few years younger than me, there was much that was still boyish about Owin.

A minute or so later I heard Alain's heavy tread come down the stairs, and put an arm across my breasts. I was in no mood or condition to be ogled by both father and son.

"Forget your modesty, Amra. There's not enough of you for me. I like my women with a little meat on their bones. And I like 'em tender, not tenderized."

I glared at him, but he didn't seem to notice.

"Great Gorm, but something got hold of you. You've got bruises on your bruises. Is that a claw mark?"

"No, it's a pimple."

Myra glanced up at her husband. "Make yourself useful and put water on to boil. Then bring me the tincture your cousin gave us, the one for unclean cuts, and that horse liniment you're always going on about. Then get me one of Owin's old shirts, in the cupboard at the top of the stairs. And then go take care of the custom."

"All right. But what about breakfast?" He cast an eye at the half-cooked bacon.

"Chew your beard, old man."

Alain did as he was told while Myra cleaned the wound, and then lumbered off to the morning's work. He paused at the door and cast one last glance in my direction.

"Will trouble be following you, do you think?"

"I don't think so, but it's possible."

He nodded and pulled down a gnarled cudgel from the wall, where it hung by a leather thong on a hook. He tucked it into his wide belt and went outside.

Once all the blood was off and the wound cleaned, Myra poured a liberal amount of some cloudy, innocuous looking tincture into each of the furrows in my shoulder. Gods, it burned. When I complained, she said "Talk to me about pain after you've birthed a child. Honestly, Amra Thetys, you sound like a man, whining about a little discomfort."

There is mercy and then there is mercy, I suppose. But her hands were deft and gentle as she rubbed the liniment on. That burned too, but in a strangely cold way that wasn't entirely painful.

She helped me into Owin's old, oft-mended shirt. I swam in it. Then she demanded my trousers.

"There's no need, Myra. Nobody will notice stained trousers. The shirt is enough. I'll be on my way and out of your hair. Thank you." I made to rise, and a meaty hand pushed me back down.

"You're on your way up to Owin's room, and nowhere else. Now out of those bloody pants, Amra."

"The longer I stay here, the more likely it is I put you and your men in danger."

"And you were in no danger at all when you pulled Alain out of that rookery where they'd drugged his ale and robbed him, and were about to cut his throat. I've waited near four years to pay that bill. Now off with your pants, or I warn you, I'll have them off myself."

"Myra, my mother died twenty years ago!"

"Isin love her soul. But at least she can't see you acting the fool now."

One more knife joined the five on the table. She clucked her tongue, but otherwise made no comment. It turned out that I needed her help to get my boots off. I couldn't bend down that far.

~ ~ ~

I slept like the dead. Through the day, and into the night. I think the only reason I woke was because I was so hungry. I was disoriented for a moment, surrounded by Owin's things, in Owin's bed. I reached for a knife that wasn't where it was supposed to be. It was a spare looking room, lit only by moonlight. A cloak hung on a peg. There was a pitcher and a bowl on a rickety stand, and a razor with a leather strop. There was a solid-looking wardrobe. There was a low table by the window, with little carvings resting on it. Creakily, I picked one up and studied it in the moonlight. It was a horse. It was beautiful. It wasn't something Owin would have bought, I didn't think. I suspected he had carved it himself. He had a master's eye, if I was right. He'd carved it in such a way that the grain of the wood flowed and accented the mane, the powerful haunches. I picked up another, a kestrel perched on a branch. It was just as lovely. He'd caught the air of regal, predatory menace in its eyes perfectly. I wondered if he even knew he was wasting a rare talent on building and repairing wagons. Or if he cared. I'd have traded the damned golden toad for one of his carvings in a trice.

The stairs were a challenge. I kept one hand on the wall and the other on my ribs. The sounds of laughter and good-natured bickering floated up from the kitchen, but they trailed off as I descended.

Owin was studiously not looking at my bare legs. Alain leaned back in his chair, mirth still lingering in his eyes. Myra glanced at me and said "Good, you're up. I was going to wake you soon, just to get some food down your throat." And she busied herself readying me a plate. I wasn't going to argue. Myra could cook. Of course, I would have eaten boot leather had it been presented to me just then.

I sat down and a plate was put in front of me. If anyone was expecting conversation out of me just then, they were sorely disappointed. Beans, capon, black bread, boiled cloudroot with a rich mushroom gravy. I made it all disappear. I looked up. Myra was smiling, Owin stared, mouth agape, and Alain just shook his head.

"What? You've never seen anyone eat?"

"Is that what you call it?" asked Alain. "No one was going to take it away from you, you know. Did you have time to taste anything?"

"Leave her alone," said Myra. "She's complimented the cook in her way."

Alain snorted, but laid off me. He changed the subject.

"Someone's been asking after you around town."

I froze, spoon halfway to my mouth. "Violent type?"

"No."

"Half-grown kid? Bald? Penitent's robes?"

He laughed. "Not hardly. But you do know all types, eh?"

I growled. "Just tell me."

"Young woman. Very pretty. Very, very pretty."

"A strumpet," injected Myra.

"A pretty strumpet. There's a thought."

"Black hair, green eyes, quality clothes."

"I don't know any—" Wait. That girl from the Dream. Estra's girl. "What's she want?" Estra knew how to get hold of me if she needed to. Why was this girl wandering around asking after me?

Alain shrugged. "She's put it about that there's a package for you at Locquewood's shop."

"I've no idea what it's about, and I don't have time for, ah, strumpets at the moment," I said, glancing at Myra, who rolled her eyes.

Owin cleared the dishes and then Myra shooed both men out of the kitchen to check my wounds. She changed the bandages on my shoulder, applying that damned tincture once more, and rubbed in more liniment. Then she brought down a parcel from a shelf, frowning. Inside were my knives, a pair of trousers she'd obviously taken in for me, my old belt, cloth for bandages, another bottle of the tincture of torture and a jar of the horse liniment. My boots were cleaned and by the door. She helped me dress, and watched with disapproving eyes while I put various knives in various places. She was the first person who'd ever seen that particular ritual.

Myra stood in front of me, hands on heavy hips, and glared. "I've done what I can. I forced some rest and food on you—well, maybe the food wasn't forced—and I've tended your wounds. I know I can't keep you longer. You're like a damned cat, Amra. If I drag you in from the rain, you'll just yowl to be let back out."

"Myra—"

"You just be quiet until I'm done. I like you, Amra, and I owe you for my man's life. You're decent and kind, however hard you may be. But I don't approve of what you do or how you live your life. Alain is the stubbornest man I ever met save my own father, yet even he doesn't usually go looking for trouble. You're going to end up dead in an alley, Amra Thetys, or swinging by your neck in Harad's Square. But it doesn't have to be that way. There's a place for you under this roof, whenever you want it. But you have to want it. Now go."

I gave the big woman a brief hug, then left. Maybe ten, twelve years ago I could have taken her up on her offer. When I was cutting purses and stealing bread to survive. Now? It was far too late for me to think of taking up any other trade, living any other life. What would I do? Marry Owin, maybe, have children, tend to the kitchen and the washing and the finances?

No, Myra. Thank you, but no. It was a good, safe, honest life you offered. But it wasn't the life for me. Not anymore. Not for a long, long time. But as I slipped out of Alain's work yard and into the night, I remembered the laughter and the amused squabbling that floated up from the kitchen table as I'd come down the stairs. And I realized there was a hole in my life, a place where a family was supposed to fit. Like a missing tooth. Or a severed limb.

CHAPTER 11

The next couple of days were spent recuperating. I didn't go home, or anywhere near my usual haunts. Instead I stayed in one of my bolt holes, a third-floor garret way the hells and gone across the river in Markgie's Rest, not even in Lucernis proper. It was a sleepy little community of fishermen and caravanners perched on the north shore of the Bay. People minded their own business, and were used to comings and goings at odd hours. And it got a breeze off the ocean most of the day.

The first day was pleasant enough. I was just too sore to want to move. By the end of the second, I was bored out of my skull. So I went down to the neighborhood pub to have a drink and be alone, in company. It was pleasant in the late afternoon, sunlight pouring in through real glass windows, surrounded by dark polished wood and red and green painted tables. I'd been there once or twice before. The few customers were mostly old men, telling amusing lies about fish and women.

I'd been there maybe half an hour when the door opened and three men walked in, bringing a Kerf-damned lot of trouble with them.

Two were your typical toughs; hard men, armed with short swords and dirks. Their clothes were clean and of good quality, and they were both clean shaven. Hard eyes scanned the crowd, and their hands never strayed too far from weapon hilts. Maybe a cut above the typical tough. Armsmen. Hired blades.

The third man was something else altogether. Slightly hunchbacked, with long, greasy black hair and a sparse beard, he wore cloth of expensive cut, but there were old stains and new on his velvet tunic. One foot was twisted in, and every step looked like it pained and exhausted him. And it looked as though he'd been walking all day. In one hand he carried a fine knife; black handled and silver pommeled, the bright blade about a hand span long and three fingers wide. A knife I knew very well. I'd commissioned it, after all. It was the knife I'd lost at the Elamner's villa.

I'd sat at a bench in the corner, back against the wall. Now I was trapped.

Hunchback, who was almost certainly Bosch, slapped the knife flat onto an empty table and stared at it. The two toughs gripped the hilts of their swords. I slipped knives into both hands and quietly pushed myself back from the table.

Nothing happened for a moment. Then the knife began to tremble. Slowly it began to turn, to spin, until the tip pointed directly at me like a Kerf-damned compass pointing north. Hunchback looked me in the eye and smiled a nasty, yellow-toothed smile that spoke volumes, all of it to do with imminent harm coming my way.

I threw both blades simultaneously, one at each bully-boy, vaulted onto the table, and threw myself through the glass of the window, arm across my face. Before I hit, I heard one of the men yelp in pain. Then I was rolling on the cobbles outside. I heard a horse's shrill neighing, looked up as a shod hoof came down towards my face. I rolled aside just in time. I'd come crashing out just as a hack was passing.

There were two more sell-swords waiting outside, but it took them a second to react. I wasted no time. I was on my feet and down the street. I didn't bother to look back. I could hear the heavy slap of boot leather on cobbles behind me.

Maybe I could have outrun them. Probably I could have. But to what point? They'd follow me wherever I went. My knife would point them the way. My three knives, now. Damned magic. For once the phrase 'you can run but you can't hide' had some meaning. So I turned three right corners in quick succession, making a square, and came back at a sprint to the tavern. My abused muscles complained bitterly, but Hunchback was right where I'd figured he would be, lagging far behind. And far away from his toughs. Sometimes I'm so smart I amaze myself.

I came up behind him in a quiet rush and put my blade across his windpipe. He stiffened. I plucked my other knife out of his hand and said,

"Where are the other two?"

"Right here. In my belt." So they were. I relieved him of those as well. I heard running footsteps rounding the corner. I spun him around to face the toughs. "Quick now, tell them to put down their swords." He hesitated, and I slid the sharp end of my blade across his stubbled neck, just enough to sting.

"Stay back! Put down your swords!" He had a cultured voice. It sounded odd coming from his twisted, dissolute body. When they hesitated, he shouted "Do as I say!" They did, breathing hard, murder in the eyes of the one I'd stuck. "Good boy," I murmured in his ear. "Now tell 'em to go inside the tavern and count to a hundred. Not too fast. I'll be counting too, and I'm not so good at it. Sometimes I lose my place and have to start again. If they come out before I'm done counting I'll cut your throat." He did as he was told, and they did what he told them, and I said "good boy" again as I dragged him down the street, and into the mouth of the nearest alley. Four pairs of eyes followed our progress from tavern door and window.

"You must be Bosch." I said as we went.

He hesitated, then nodded. Carefully.

"Out of curiosity, where'd you find my knife?"

"In a planter in the garden."

"The one place I didn't think to look. Tell the Elamner he'd better back off if he doesn't want the toad melted down." I thought it best not to mention the corpse I'd seen. I still hadn't figured out what the hells it signified.

"You have the statue?"

"No, I just assumed your boss would want a golden toad. Doesn't everybody?"

"We can do business, then."

"Yes," I said. "We can deal."

"How shall we contact you?"

I yanked out a handful of his hair and pushed him into the gutter. I tucked the hair into the top of a boot.

"Don't worry. I'll find you." And then I turned and tried to make myself scarce. I was sure Holgren would know just what to do with Bosch's greasy locks.

It wasn't Bosch's men that got me. It was the Watch. Markgie's Rest wasn't the Rookery, or Silk Street. When taverns got busted up and blood got spilled, and people started running around in the street with bared blades, they came. In large numbers. Quickly.

There was nowhere for me to go. Three appeared ahead of me, and two more behind, blocking off the alley. Black, varnished billys thunked into meaty palms. One old codger with a mean eye had a crossbow and looked like he knew how to use it. Blank walls rose on either side.

"Kerf's shrivelled balls," I spat, and dropped my knife, and put out my hands.

They beat me unconscious anyway.

CHAPTER 12

When I came back to the world, I wished I hadn't.

The smell was awful. Piss and vomit and shit and fear. The stench of bodies that had forgotten what clean water was, much less soap. To draw breath was to gag. I couldn't see anything. The darkness was absolute. I felt rough straw and filth-slick stone under my cheek, heard distant screams echoing along stone corridors. Somewhere not far away a hoarse, gravelly voice kept moaning 'Mother? Mother?' in such a monotonous way that I could hear the madness behind it.

I groaned and began the slow, torturous process of levering myself up off the floor. Everything hurt. When I put my hand out to work myself into a sitting position, I planted it squarely into a pile of cold, runny feces.

"Welcome to Havelock Prison," I whispered to myself. "Mind the turds."

~ ~ ~

In the darkness it was impossible to gauge the passing of time. My cell was three paces by four, and the ceiling higher than I could reach with outstretched arms. The door was oak banded in iron, and had been gouged futilely by unknown numbers of former occupants. All the stonework was tight; there were no chinks that I could find by fingertip, though someone at some time had made a concerted if futile effort to loosen a stone in the back-right corner. The stones around it were gouged and rough. A thin layer of fouled, louse-ridden straw lined the floor. I kicked it all into a corner. After a time, I stopped noticing the stench, and started noticing the lice.

All my knives were gone, of course. In the darkness I felt carefully in my boot, and came up with a single strand of Bosch's hair. I didn't see how it would do me any good now, but I wound it carefully around the back of a button on my shirt, just in case.

The wound on my shoulder ached abominably. Nothing I could do about that, or the fact that it would probably become infected in such a foul environment. Not that it mattered, really; if they had me this far down in the bowels of Havelock, I probably wasn't coming back up for anything other than a dance with the noose.

~ ~ ~

After an unknowable time, I noticed a creeping light coming from under the door. I heard muffled orders repeated at regular intervals, and sometimes blows and shouts of pain. By the time they arrived at my door, I knew the drill.

"Face against the back wall, hands on your head, eyes shut. You have until five. One. Two. Three. Four. Five." Then a bar was lifted and the door swung open. Even turned away with my eyes closed, the flickering torchlight was dazzling.

From the sounds, there were at least two, possibly three. Probably three. One to hold the torch, one to serve the food, and one to stand ready with the billy. I didn't make any trouble. I'd had enough beatings for a while. The light retreated, the door closed, the bar slammed home.

My first meal in Havelock was gruel; stale, poorly ground rye bread; and water that, from the taste and smell of it, had most likely been drawn straight from the Ose.

To this day, just a whiff of rye bread is enough to make my stomach turn.

~ ~ ~

Mother-man, as I came to think of him, was never truly quiet. Even in his sleep he would moan for her. I assume he was sleeping. And when he woke, he'd scream "Mother! I'm blind! Moooother!" On and on until they came to beat him quiet. Then, at most a few hours later, he'd start again with that monotonous call for maternal comfort.

Eventually I couldn't stand it anymore. I screamed at him, "Your whore of a mother is dead, shit brain. Shut it!" It only made him go on louder. Which made me invent ever more gruesome ends for her. Run over by a carriage. Gored by bulls, made into meat pies. Drowned in a cesspit. Gnawed to death by rats, face first. Dead of syphilis. It only made him carry on the louder, which made the guards come. They beat us both.

I found myself hoping they'd come to hang either him or me soon. I started not to care which.

~ ~ ~

My second meal was the same as the first, and my third. That was how I measured time, though I honestly couldn't have said at the time if we were fed every day or every other or at random intervals. Hunger warred with nausea, and time had no meaning.

I thought a lot. Not much else to do. I went over the entire situation, and realized they might just be holding me until the killers arrived from Courune. They'd probably want to question me before they took me to Harad's Square for my short drop into oblivion. I didn't think they would be gentle about the questions, either.

I also thought about the situation as a whole. I went over everything I knew, and everything I thought I knew. I didn't reach any new conclusions. I still thought the Elamner must have had Corbin killed, for the statue. There were thirteen, Corbin had said. Heirus or Bosch had gotten twelve, and still wanted the last, the toad, so the others must not have been terribly important to him. Not what he was looking for, perhaps. Which suggested he knew when he commissioned Corbin that the one he was looking for was in that temple, but he didn't know which one it was. Or maybe he just needed all of them.

As for the dead man in the villa, well, that reeked of magic. By its nature, magic makes no sense. It was possible Bosch had killed his boss and was running the whole show. It was equally possible that the dead man wasn't the Elamner at all. I just didn't have enough to go on to make any kind of conclusion. Didn't matter. If I ever got out, I just needed to hunt down Bosch and make him talk. Then I'd see who needed to be killed.

The thing that had tried to break into my apartment and left me alive at the Elamner's was also a cipher. Was it working for Heirus, or Bosch? Or was it something completely Other? No idea. I'd ask Bosch about that, too, next time I saw him.

After a time it all became a muddle in my mind, and I tried not to think at all. And then they finally came for me, and all I could think of was how I didn't want to die.

They put the manacles on, and the shackles, and I shuffled out of my hole with a billy in my back down a stone corridor, eyes watering at the light from the torch behind me and the smoky corridor. We went up a set of stairs, and down another corridor. This one was lit, and the cell doors had barred windows. Pale, emaciated faces stared out at us, but they were just blurs in the increased light. There was nothing wrong with my ears, though. And these prisoners hadn't seen a woman in a long time.

"Bring 'er in 'ere for five minutes before she swings! All right, three! Three minutes!"

"Just keep walking," said one of the guards behind me. I gritted my teeth and kept shuffling along.

"She shouldn't go to the gallows unsatisfied!"

"Let me impale her before you hang her!"

I kept walking, until somebody threw a handful of runny shit that hit me in the face. Then I lunged at the bastard. The guard slammed me in the kidney with his billy and I crumpled to the floor.

"Told you to keep walking." He looked down at me and sighed. His partner put his torch in an empty bracket.

"Yeah," I gasped. "I forgot."

"You won't forget again?"

"Not a chance."

"Well, everybody forgets every now and then, I suppose. You stay right there for a while."

"Not going anywhere."

He looked at his partner, who nodded.

"Gerard, I told you last time. You start throwing shit, and I'm going to make you eat it."

"No boss. I forgot, boss."

"That's what you said the last time, Gerard." And he lifted the bar to

Gerard's door.

"No boss! She forgot! Everybody forgets, you said so!"

"I'm just going to help your memory along, Gerard."

They opened the shit-flinger's door and beat him senseless. And yes, by the end of it he had shit in his mouth. I won't say I liked them for it. But I certainly didn't feel bad for Gerard. In prison, I discovered, the only pity to be had was self-pity.

CHAPTER 13

They brought me to a lantern-lit room. There was a scarred wooden table. There were two chairs, both facing me on the opposite side of the table. There was a door behind the table, opposite the one they'd brought me through. They ran a chain through my manacles and locked it to a massive iron staple in the stone floor, and then they stood back, within billy-swinging distance. And then we waited. Slowly my watering eyes adjusted to the light.

After maybe five minutes the door opened and two men walked in. The first I recognized. Inspector Kluge. The second I'd never seen before.

He was a heavy, unlovely man. Deeply inset dark eyes that glittered in the lamplight. Close-cropped, receding, greying hair. Heavy, pockmarked face and thin lips. A small scar bisected one of his thick eyebrows. But he was immaculate. His wide, square nails were clean and manicured. He wore an embroidered black waistcoat over a pure white linen shirt, and his starched collar was buttoned right up to his jaw line, biting slightly into the loose skin of his neck. This man had money, was used to money. He said nothing, only took a seat and looked at me. His face was impassive.

Kluge sat on the edge of the table nearest me. He scanned a sheaf of papers that he'd brought into the room.

"You put a knife into a man's arm, and you put another knife to another man's neck. You destroyed a rather expensive tavern window. The tavern keeper will want recompense. The injured and threatened parties did not care to prefer charges, but the crown does not require them to, in order to try you for a violent crime, Amra Thetys. Or do you still prefer Marfa?"

"Amra is fine."

He put the papers aside and looked at me for a long while.

"We know who you are. We know what you are. The only reason you don't yet have a date with the hangman is because we believe you can assist us."

"You'd hang me for a tavern brawl?"

"No. For that you could spend three years in Havelock. By the time you got out, you would be toothless from the poor diet, and your body would be wasted from malnutrition. Your eyesight would probably never recover from the dark hole you'd be consigned to. You might perhaps become a charwoman. Or you could sell scraps of salvaged cloth down in Temple Market. That is the best you could hope for, Amra.

"If you swing, it will be either for theft, or for aiding in the murder of a noble. It doesn't really matter. If we want you to hang, you'll hang."

I nodded. I didn't doubt what he said. Any of it.

"Well, then, I can't think of anything I'd rather do than help you, Inspector Kluge."

He smiled. "I knew you were a sensible creature." He stood and motioned to the other, silent man. "May I present to you Lord Osskil det Thracen-Courune. Corbin's elder brother."

"I'd bow, or curtsey. If I knew how, and if I could." I rattled the chains. He ignored it.

"I am going to ask you questions," Lord Osskil said, "and you are going to answer immediately, and without prevarication. Do you understand?"

"Certainly. I have an expansive vocabulary."

"Did you have anything to do with the death of my brother?"

"No."

"Do you know who did?"

"Yes."

"Tell me who."

"I don't think so."

The guard was quick with his billy. He slammed it into the back of my thigh and I went sprawling. Chained, I couldn't raise my hands, and so I broke my fall with my face.

"Get up," said Kluge. I worked my way to my feet, nose bleeding and probably broken.

Osskil asked again. "Who is responsible for my brother's death?"

"Before I answer, do you mind if I share a few thoughts?"

A short silence, pregnant with violence. Then, "Why not," he said, face expressionless.

"If I tell you now, what's to stop you from sending me right back into that hole?"

"If you don't tell us," said Kluge, "you will certainly go back into that hole. Until they take you to Harad's Square."

I nodded. "Maybe so, maybe no. But the man who killed Corbin might never be caught then."

Silence reigned. Then Osskil spoke up. "Tell me what I want to know, and I guarantee you will go free once the murderer has been punished."

"Release me and I'll take you to the bastard."

The guard reared back to smack me down again, but Osskil raised his hand.

"I'm curious about you, Amra Thetys. Who was my brother to you?"

"A friend. A colleague, so to speak."

"Were you lovers?"

I laughed. "No, Lord Osskil. Your brother and I weren't lovers."

"What were you doing there, at that house? Where they found the body."

"I went to look for him. He was supposed to stop by my house about midnight. When he didn't show up, I started to worry, so I went looking for him."

"Why were you worried?"

I suppose I could have lied. But I didn't see the point.

"Look, you know your brother was a thief. He was a good one, if that means anything to you. He stole some things for someone, and they tried to stiff him his commission. He was going to meet them that night to settle the account. They weren't nice people. He asked me to look after his damned dog if he didn't show up by morning."

Kluge sniffed. "What you aren't saying is louder than what you are, Amra."

I shook my head. "Fine. He'd acquired a lot of statues for his client, and they'd taken all but one from him and neglected to pay him. But that one they missed? They wanted it badly, or so he said. He was supposed to meet and discuss his payment. It was going to be substantially higher than originally agreed to. He called it a bad faith penalty or some such. Obviously he went to the meet, and ran into more bad faith."

"Why did he go to you at all? Did he want help?"

"No. He wanted me to hold onto the last statue for him. I turned him down. I didn't want the risk. But I did agree to look after his dog should anything go wrong." I hoped the one lie would go unnoticed amidst all the truth.

Kluge changed the topic. "Tell me about the fight in the tavern, Amra."

"What about it?"

"Witnesses say you drew steel and attacked without any provocation. Three men walk in, you throw a knife into one man's arm and then throw yourself out the window."

"Is there a question in there?"

"Why did you attack three men, two of which were obviously swordsmen, without provocation?"

"I owed them money. They'd come to collect, and I didn't have it."

"If that was all there was to it, I might believe you. But then you lead them on a chase and return to the tavern, and hold up the man who seems to be the employer of the group. You threatened him."

"I wanted him to cancel my debt."

"Mages aren't generally in the business of loaning money to thieves. Or anyone."

"He was a mage? I doubt he was a powerful one. Well, you'd know better than I, Inspector Kluge. But I don't see why mages can't take up any line of work they want. Loan sharking. Even detective work."

He smiled a tight smile. "I think the two incidents are connected. I think those men had something to do with Corbin Hardin's death. I think you tried to brace the killer, perhaps to blackmail money for your silence, and it went awry."

"And I think I should be half a foot taller, and rich as Borkin Breaves. Thinking something doesn't make it so."

"But if I think it, Amra, if I think it strongly enough, you hang. So if I'm wrong, it falls on you to convince me of the truth."

I sighed. I ached, I was tired, I was hungry. A wave of dizziness came over me. "Do you mind if I sit?" I asked, and started to squat. One of the guards put a billy under my chin and lifted.

"Let her," said Osskil. And the club went away.

"You are too kind, lord." I got as comfortable as I could. Osskil stood up and dragged his chair around the table.

"You might not want to get too close," said Kluge.

"I don't believe she's much of a threat. She can barely stand."

I chuckled. "It's not me you have to worry about, Lord Osskil. It's the lice."

He stiffened a little. "Oh," was all he said. He set his chair down a couple of feet from me and settled in it, leaning forward to look in my eyes.

"If I give you my word you will be freed, will you tell me who killed my brother?"

I considered. He could probably be trusted. Nobles were generally particular about keeping their word. I shook my head, though.

"You don't believe I can be trusted?"

"It's not that. There's another problem."

"What other problem?"

"I swore I'd kill the bastard myself. If you go and do it, then what's my word worth?"

He just stared at me for a moment, and then he laughed. I suppose the idea of a thief worried about keeping her word was funny at that. I just waited it out.

Eventually his laugher trailed off into silence.

"You're serious, aren't you?"

"You think only nobles do what they say they will?"

"No. Most of my peers wouldn't think twice about breaking an oath. But why would you care about honor?"

"If you have to ask, you wouldn't understand. Let me ask you a question, if I may."

"Why not," he said again in that curiously flat manner of his.

"When was the last time you saw your brother? Alive, I mean."

His face went impassive. I began to suspect that's what he looked like when he was deciding whether to be angry.

"Why?"

"Because in all the time I knew Corbin, he never mentioned you. He spoke of his daughter, a little. Once he mentioned his wife, when he was drunk. But he never mentioned his old man, and he never talked about a brother."

"What are you getting at?"

"Just this. For the past three years I've drunk with Corbin, eaten with him, laughed with him and once or twice I even cried with him. If I'd wanted it, I could have slept with him, though gods only know why he wanted to, considering the mess I've made of my face over the years. But I thought at the time it would just complicate our friendship.

"We watched each other's back, and bragged to each other about scores. We lent each other money and we bet on the horses, and the cards, and the dice. The day before he died, he asked me to look after his dog. And the morning he died, I had to pull that howling mutt away from the smell of his blood. I'm the one that got to tell his lover that he'd died, and how. But somehow I'm the one who's chained to a floor, and you're the one laughing when I say I'm going to kill the man who did it."

I shook my head. I was a little bitter. "Life's a funny thing, when you think about it, lord."

"You think I didn't love my brother?" I heard a hint of roughness in his voice.

"I have no idea."

"You're right. You don't. The Corbin you knew was a different man."

"That's my point exactly. The man whose death you came to avenge was already dead. I don't know who killed Corbin Hardin det Thracen-Courune. I *do* know who killed Corbin Hardin, the thief. That's who I have a score to settle with. Who do you have a score with, Lord Osskil?"

His face paled. I thought he was going to hit me, but he stood up and turned away. The silence stretched on and on. Osskil broke it first.

"Let her go, Kluge."

"My lord, I hardly think—"

"I said let her go free. Do it now."

"But Lord Osskil—"

"Do not make me say it a third time, Inspector."

"As you wish, my lord."

Osskil stuck out his hand. I didn't know what he wanted at first. Then I got it. I put my hand in his and he hauled me up. He didn't even wipe it, afterward.

"Amra, I am lodging at the Thracen manse, on the Promenade. I hope you will call on me, that I may be of assistance to you in your... endeavor.

Corbin's funeral is tomorrow at noon, at the Necropolis. You are welcome to attend." And he walked out, just like that. Kluge trailed after him, snapping out a 'release her' over his shoulder.

The guards undid the chain, the shackles, the manacles. The one who had made Gerard eat shit said, "You must have struck a nerve."

"I guess so."

"You want some advice? You walk out the gates, you keep walking 'till you get to the docks. Then you board a boat. The first one away. Because as soon as this lord leaves town, Kluge will round you up. And next time, you won't never see the light of day again."

CHAPTER 14

They kept my knives. Said they were misplaced, along with all my coin. I wasn't particularly surprised. I walked down an arched corridor to a huge set of double doors. The guard opened a pedestrian door cut into the huge left-hand gate, and the sunlight streaming in made my eyes water. The world was a blur. Street traffic was a howling din. How had I never noticed how loud Lucernis was before?

Slowly my eyes adjusted, and I set off. Three blocks from Havelock I saw a signboard featuring a straight razor and a spray of whitehearts. As soon as I walked in to the barber, a booming voice assaulted my sensitive ears.

"Oy! Out with you. No beggars in 'ere!" He was absurdly tall, and thin as a stick, and his waxed, bald head reflected the morning light. He was making shooing gestures. Probably because he could smell me from across the room. I was his only customer besides an old man dozing on a bench.

I leaned against the doorframe and lifted my left foot. I pulled and twisted the heel of my boot until it swung out, revealing the little cavity I'd paid extra for. I pulled out three gold marks and flipped one to the barber.

"My name is Dorn," he said. "Welcome to my shop, mister...?"

"Since I barely look human, I won't take offense to that."

He colored. "Don't do women."

I flipped him the other marks. I'd just given him what he'd make in a month. More than a month. "For that much you will."

"Always thought I'd been missing out on half my custom, sticking to men. What would you like today, miss?"

"If I don't get clean very, very soon, I'm going to kill someone. I'm going to need a bath. No, two baths. With hot water. Not cold, not tepid. Boiling hot. I'll need new clothes and food. No gruel, no water, and no Kerf-damned rye bread. Wine, lots of it. And I have *got* to get rid of these lice. Do you have anything for that?"

"That really works, you mean?"

"Yes."

He smiled, and brought out his straight razor. "It's not just the lice. It's the nits. And they make their home down at the roots of yer hair."

"Shit."

~ ~ ~

I stepped out of Dorn's shop four hours later, in new clothes, fed, bald, and vaguely human. The only things that hadn't gone into the fire were my boots and Bosch's single strand of hair. I still itched, but was fairly certain I had been thoroughly deloused and de-nitted. My new look drew stares. One passing matron looked at me with something akin to horror in her eyes. I was going to have to get a hat.

"Should have seen me before," I told her. She hurried off. And I did the same.

~ ~ ~

When I reached out to unlock my door, a wispy face materialized in the wood grain, opened its eyes and said "Amra." I shrieked and reached for where a knife should have been.

"Holgren is coming. Stay here." Then it disappeared. Damned magic.

I unlocked the normal-once-more door and slipped inside.

My place was thoroughly, unutterably destroyed. Someone with a lot of time and patience had taken everything apart. Every pillow was ripped open, every stick of furniture was in splinters. My clothing was charred rags in the grate. Floorboards were pried up and paintings slashed. Delicate glasswork was halfway back to the sand it had been made from. If someone had given me two pennies for the whole lot, they would have overpaid.

I checked my hidey-hole. They had found that, too. Empty. That was a good chunk of my money gone.

They'd missed two good knives and one bottle of terrible wine. That was it. That was all I had left, besides a little money on deposit with a moneylender who didn't care about the provenance of his customers' coin. That, and my very, very well protected retirement money, which I had promised myself I'd never touch until I got too old to do what I do.

Oh, well. After Havelock, I was much less upset than I might otherwise have been. Prison, I found, was wonderful for clarifying your priorities. I cleared some of the debris from a corner and sat down with my bottle to wait for Holgren.

He walked through the door less than an hour later. Holgren didn't bother with knocking. Or locks, for that matter. He took a look around, one eyebrow raised.

"Did you upset the housekeeper?"

"Ha ha. Somebody turned the place while I was in prison."

"You were in prison?"

"Don't remind me. Wine?" I held out the bottle.

"Is it any good?"

"The very best I have."

He took a sip. Swallowed, reluctantly. "That's ghastly."

"True." I took another swig. "Tell me, how is it that everybody in Lucernis seems to know where I live, when I haven't told anybody?"

He shrugged, paused. "Ah, Amra?"

"Yes?"

"What in Gorm's name have you done to your hair?"

"It's the latest fashion. You don't like it?'

"I'd always assumed *hair* was an integral part of any hairstyle."

"Sure, insult my home, my wine and my looks, why don't you."

"What are friends for?"

That took me aback a little. Holgren was likeable enough for a mage, and I trusted him to a certain degree, but friends? I don't make friends easily.

"What did you want, anyway?"

"It's about that toad you left with me. Actually, it's about what's inside the toad."

"I'll bite. What's inside the toad?"

"I'm not exactly sure."

The thing about Holgren, he doesn't realize when he's being frustratingly cryptic. Probably doesn't.

"There's a vein that throbs in your forehead. I've never noticed that before. Your hair must have hidden it."

"Will you tell me what's so important about the unspecified thing in the toad?"

"Oh. Well, that's just it. I want to melt it down. To find out."

"I might need the toad. As a bargaining chip." Actually, I was surprised he'd thought to wait for my permission.

"Whatever is inside, it's ancient. Definitely pre-Diaspora. And it's powerful, Amra. The most powerful artefact I've ever personally run across."

Pre-Diaspora meant that whatever it was, it was more than a thousand years old. Possibly much, much more. From the Age of Gods. From humanity's first cultures, before the Cataclysm that killed millions and saw the survivors fleeing for their lives. The time of the Diaspora, when the gods went mad and the race of man ran screaming in every direction, abandoning an entire continent. An age of myth and legend. And powerful and deadly artefacts.

"How powerful are we talking, Holgren?"

"I believe the thing inside the statuette is, in some way, self-aware. Probably intelligent, possibly even alive."

"Magical, then."

"Yes. But not human magic. I suspect that whatever it is, it was god-forged."

"And you want to let it out of the toad? Doesn't that strike you as a tad dangerous? I seem to recall you saying something like it being 'dangerous and distasteful.'"

He shrugged. "What can I say? I've always been the curious sort."

"You mages are all mad."

"Don't oversimplify, Amra. So?"

"So what?"

"Do I have your permission?"

I sighed. "Why not?"

"Good. I'd tell you to pack your things, but I suspect there's nothing to pack."

The first faint stirrings of suspicion started to claw their way through my guts. "Why should I want to pack?"

"Well you can't stay here, can you? Not with the contract and all."

My blood went cold. Suspicion blossomed into dread. "What contract?" I said in as calm a voice as I could muster.

"I didn't tell you? Someone's put a thousand-mark bounty out on you. Or your corpse, rather, but only if it's intact."

"What? When?"

"Two days ago, I think. Yes, two. Must have slipped my mind."

"How does something like that slip your Kerf-damned mind?"

He seemed slightly affronted. "Well they aren't after me, now are they? Don't worry. You'll come stay with me. It's the safest place for you. That I guarantee."

"Do you have any idea what people will do for that kind of money, Holgren?"

"Oh yes. Almost anything. But attacking a mage in his own sanctum is unlikely to be one of them."

"Why my whole corpse?" I wondered. But I already had an idea.

"I can only assume they're able to use necromantic measures to extract information. Such measures require the body to be intact to a great degree."

"They want the toad."

"They want the toad," he agreed.

I put my head in my hands. I was tired. I had sworn to kill Corbin's murderer, but I didn't see how I was going to do that, since I was going to be busy dodging every back alley tough with a blade, club, rock or heavy fist. I would be looking over my shoulder every second, and waiting for assassins in my sleep.

"I should leave Lucernis."

"For that much money, there will be assassins following you to any city on the Dragonsea. Anyone who vaguely matches your description is likely to get a knife in the heart. Your best course of action is to find and deal with whoever offered the contract. Or you could match the offer, I suppose."

"Oh, sure. Can you turn around for a minute while I pull a thousand marks out of my arse?" I meant it as sarcasm, but it gave me an idea. A costly idea, but an idea.

"It was just a thought. No need to get ugly."

"Well having a price on my head hasn't improved my mood." I took a deep breath.

"We will get it all sorted, Amra. You'll see. Come, let's go." He stuck a hand out and helped me up.

"Holgren."

"What?"

"Why are you helping me?"

His brow furrowed. "Why shouldn't I?"

"Because I've landed in the shit wagon, and there's no way you're going to come away clean from this if you help me out."

He cracked one of his rare smiles. Well, rare in that it wasn't condescending. Not terribly condescending, anyway. "I like you, Amra. You're capable and you have two wits to rub together. You're good at what you do. And it won't hurt to have you in my debt. Reason enough?"

"Not really, no."

He laughed. "Gods above, but you're suspicious. Come on, the day is wasting, and the longer that dog is left alone, the greater the destruction is likely to be." He dug out a frayed piece of string from a pocket and handed it to me. "Tie this around your wrist."

"What is it?"

"Just a fetish. It will suggest to inquisitive eyes that they see nothing interesting. I don't want to fight a running battle through the streets of the city."

"Magic?"

"What do you think?"

"How long is this thing good for?"

"It should be effective for two or three days."

"How effective is it? How does it work, exactly?"

"That depends. Anyone who knows you well won't be discomfited. They'll see you just as you are. To anyone who doesn't know you, you'll be just another face in the crowd. An unremarkable one. But any physical contact will negate the effects."

"What about if I just talk to someone?"

"Well, the longer you converse, the less effective it will be. Passing pleasantries won't violate the spell. A heated discussion will."

"How much do you charge for something like this?"

"If I sold such things, I imagine I could make fifty marks or so. But I don't sell my ability, Amra. At least not directly."

"Why the hells not?"

"I just don't."

I shut up, being able to take a hint when it suited me. I tied the string on to my wrist one-handed, tightening the knot with my teeth. And then we were off.

I knew Holgren's fetish was the real thing by the time we'd got to Daughter's Bridge and not a single person had taken a second look at me despite my bald head. Holgren was a damned good mage. Made me wonder yet again why he chose to steal for a living.

~ ~ ~

Despite his professed curiosity, Holgren seemed in no rush to melt down the toad. I had expected him to toss it in a crucible and stoke the fire. Instead he rambled on about some series of preparations involving the laying of wards and whatnot. I had no idea what he was talking about, and frankly didn't much care about the details.

"How long?" I asked him.

"A day, perhaps two. Likely two. I want to take care."

"Good. I want to be around to see what's inside, Kerf knows why. But I have some errands to run. You sure this bracelet is good for another day or so?"

"If any knives sprout from your back I'll give you a full refund."

"Comforting."

"When you come back, don't bother knocking. The door knows you now, and I won't want to be disturbed."

"All right. But you should really get some rest. You look like three miles of bad road. When was the last time you slept?"

He waved that away. I wanted to ask him about Bosch's hair, but he was so wrapped up in what he was doing that I didn't. It would wait. I wasn't in any rush to confront Bosch again. As I was slipping out the door, Holgren looked up from the tome he was studying.

"Amra?"

"Yeah?"

"Be careful."

"Always."

CHAPTER 15

Fengal Daruvner had been my fixer and fence almost as long as I'd been in Lucernis. I'd met him within weeks of stepping off the boat. He had given me my first contract. He'd always been fair and trustworthy, within the limits of his own self-interest. I'd brought him a lot of swag over the years. We put meat on each other's tables.

He was a large round man with the red cheeks and nose of someone who likes his drink. He never picked up a glass before noon, and never put one down after. Behind his jolly, fatherly banter was a sharp mind. He'd survived a long time on the wrong side of the law, and he'd made so few enemies as to barely count. And those he did make ended up at the bottom of the Ose, like as not. He knew everyone, and everyone knew him. He was part of the fabric of the city. Or at least the undercity.

He ran a rank eatery on Third Wall Road. The best thing that could be said about the food was that it was cheap, and the portions were huge. I found him there, ensconced at his table in the back. His runner, a kid named Kettle because of his girth, sat behind him, dozing. Daruvner had one of his nieces on his knee, telling her some outrageous story. I couldn't remember which one she was. There were five and they all looked alike except for a bit of height difference.

He saw me as I came through the door and waved me back. I guess that meant he knew me intimately enough for Holgren's fetish to have no effect. That, or Daruvner had his own magic. Or both. I weaved my way through the crowd of late night diners to his table.

The little girl ignored me, but then his nieces always ignored everyone but Uncle Fengal.

"Amra! I see you've got the Havelock curls! I must say it hasn't improved your looks."

"I just wanted to look more like you, Daruvner. You're always saying bald is beautiful."

"For a man, yes. For you?" He leaned back and considered. "It makes you look like a penitent. Or an ascetic. It makes you look haunted, girl. Haunted and holy."

Kettle opened one eye, winked at me, closed it again. Cheeky kid.

I sat down at Daruvner's table. "That's me," I said. "Saint Amra of the second story. Got anything to drink?"

Daruvner whispered in his niece's ear. She giggled, slid down off his knee, and ran off to the kitchen. Daruvner poured winter wine into two of the thimble-sized glasses it was meant to be drunk from.

"To your friend Corbin."

"You heard?"

"Of course."

"To Corbin," I said, and sipped appreciatively. It was a little sweet for my taste, but fine. Silence stretched a bit.

"Speaking of Corbin, I got a note from Locquewood that there's a package waiting for you at his shop."

I waved that away. "I've been indisposed. I'll sort that out when I have time."

He chuckled. "Indisposed. That's one way of putting it."

"So did you know, or just suspect?" I asked.

"About you being taken to Havelock? I found out the day after. I made some inquiries, talked to a friend who owes me a favor. There was nothing I could do for you."

"Why?"

"Because you were being held on a nobleman's order."

"No, I mean why did you try to help?"

He stared at me. Then he shook his head. Then he started laughing.

"What? Did I say something funny?"

"No. That's just it, Amra. It's not funny at all. But what can you do but laugh?"

"I have no idea what you're talking about."

"I know you don't. Otherwise I might be insulted." He downed his thimble, scratched his ample belly. Gave me a mild stare. "How long have we known each other?"

"Six, seven years?"

"Eight years, almost to the day. How many commissions have I got for you?"

"I don't know. Dozens."

"Thirty-eight commissions. All of which you have fulfilled, to the very letter. You've never held out on me and you've never double-crossed me. And when you work solo, you invariably come to me to fence anything that needs to be fenced."

"I'm sure I'm not the only one."

"Don't be so sure. The ones who are as clever as you, eventually they either get too clever and try to keep a commission for themselves, or they find out they aren't as clever as they thought, and get caught. And get dead."

"Like Corbin?"

"Like Corbin? I don't know. I don't know the details, but dead is dead. The point is you're something special. To lose you would be a blow to my business. And to me personally. So I tried to see if I could pry you out of Havelock. I couldn't, but it seems you managed to spring yourself. Though I hear that you might just have been safer inside."

"That's why I'm here."

He sighed. "I suspected as much. I have a cousin in Isinglas who can set you up. I know it isn't Lucernis, but what is?"

"No, Daruvner. It's not that. I'm not going anywhere."

He lifted his eyebrows. "Are you sure?"

"Very. I have some business that won't wait."

"So what do you need from me?"

"A name."

He shook his head. "I don't know a name, Amra. You would know better than I who'd want you dead."

"Not that name. I have a good idea who's paying. I want to know who inked the contract."

Murder for hire is a nasty business, even in law-challenged Lucernis, and treated appropriately. Every contract went through layers of intermediaries, to keep any of the nastiness from sticking. But somewhere under all those layers was someone who held the money, and wrote out the contract. I'd never had cause to wonder who that was. Until now.

"That... that could be very dangerous information, Amra. I'm not sure I should tell you. I can't see how knowing will help you at all. Quite the contrary."

I shrugged. "Let me worry about that. It will never come back to you, that I promise."

"It isn't that. It's just—these are not nice people, even for such as you and me. You are an artist in your way, and I am a businessman. But these people, they are killers. In their core, you understand?"

I smiled. "Whatever you might think I look like, I'm no saint, Fengal Daruvner. I've seen death, and caused it."

"But it isn't your trade. You don't strangle old ladies in their beds to secure inheritances. You don't knife cheating husbands, you don't hurl barren wives down flights of stairs. That sort of ruthlessness is not in you, Amra Thetys, no more than it is in me. The man attached to the name you want, he is as bad as they come."

"So you know him."

"I once saw him cut a man's throat. The poor bastard was eating his dinner, and they were laughing and chatting, and then in the blink of an eye he slit the poor sod's neck from ear to ear. And then he pushed the dying man out of the chair, sat down in it, and finished the bloody food." Daruvner shook his head. "Do you know what he said to me? He said, 'Needs more salt.'"

"What's his name, Daruvner? It's not like there's no-one else to ask."

"You won't listen, will you? His name is Gavon, then. Guache Gavon. He owns the Cock's Spur, down in the Rookery."

The Rookery was a part of Lucernis that had turned cancerous over the centuries, home only to the destitute and the desperate. Morno's reforms weren't even a rumor in its narrow, labyrinthine, garbage-choked streets, and the Watch didn't dare set foot in it. People called it the Twelfth Hell. And the Cock's Spur was one of the public houses that was considered to have a 'bad' reputation there. It didn't surprise me that the owner also had a side-line in murder for hire.

"Thank you, Fengal."

"Don't thank me for telling you something likely to get you killed."

"Fine then. But I owe you."

"Do you mean that?"

"Yes."

"Then make me a promise."

"If I can."

"Don't go alone."

"Fengal—"

"I mean it, Amra. Don't go down there without someone to watch your back. Literally. I can scare up someone capable and trustworthy if you give me a couple of hours."

"Who did you have in mind?"

"The mage. Holgren Angrado."

"He's busy right now."

One eyebrow rose.

"He's already helping me, in exchange for something you don't want to know anything about. Trust me."

"Well he's sensible enough to know I'm right about this. Don't go to the Rookery without him."

"Fengal, I'm a grown woman."

"You owe me, and you promised."

"Not yet I haven't."

"But you will."

And a quarter hour later, I did. I was tired of arguing. Daruvner usually gets what he wants, if for no other reason than he has the patience of a stone.

CHAPTER 16

I hadn't told Daruvner why I wanted Gavon's name, and he hadn't asked directly. He was too polite for that. Or he knew better than to ask questions he didn't want answers to. He suspected I planned to kill the man, to make a statement. Which had its appeal, admittedly, but it wasn't what I had planned. Would-be assassins would certainly be put off if I killed the man who inked the contract on me, but I just don't have the stomach for cold-blooded murder. Daruvner was right about that. Oh, I could argue the morality of it with myself all day, and make a perfect case for putting a knife in the heart of a man who made a living being the middleman for murderers and their clients, but I couldn't fool myself. If I had to I could do it, but I hoped I wouldn't have to.

Instead I was going to try something a little more tricky. I was counting on the fact that a fixer, even a fixer for assassins, would have to honor any contract if he wanted to stay in business.

I just hoped to Kerf that it worked. If it did, no one would dream of trying to cash in on the bounty that had been put on my head. If it didn't, I'd almost certainly be dead. Either way, my problems would be over.

But before all that, I had a funeral to attend.

~ ~ ~

The City of the Dead. From the outside it looked like some mad prince's idea of a fortress, massive white walls stretching up and up, though there were no sentry towers. I certainly wouldn't have wanted to try and scale them; they were damned-near glassy and thoroughly seamless. Besides, against all that white I would have been a tad conspicuous, whatever I wore. Also, there was no need. The gate to the Necropolis was open, unlocked, and unguarded all day long. If I ever decided it behooved me to rob the dead, I could just stroll in and hide myself in a corner somewhere until everyone left. Gods knew the place was full of nooks and crannies.

There was only one gate, a thing of impressive impracticality made of oak timbers a foot thick banded with iron and inscribed with arcane symbols that throbbed with power. Next to the gate in a half-dozen languages was a notice:

The Gate Closes Half a Glass Before Sunset.
Be Ye on the Outside Before Then.
No Littering
No Blood-Spilling
No Hurdy-Gurdy Music
No Fornication

It made me wonder. Was all of this to keep the dead safe, or the living?

Once in the gate I was surrounded by mausoleums. Some were little bigger than doll houses, others dwarfed my rented rooms. Headstones and statuary squeezed higgledy-piggledy in between.

There was one gravel path. I took it, but the task of finding Corbin's funeral was daunting. The place was a giant maze.

"It's over there, on the hill with the large, not terribly well done Weeping Mother statue."

I spun around. It was the boy in the penitent's robes.

"What is?"

"Your friend's funeral."

"Who the hells are you?"

"Arhat," he said, as if that cleared everything up.

"What do you want, Arhat?"

"To pay my respects. I... failed your friend, in a manner of speaking. I'm sorry."

"Failed him how?" I asked, but he just shook his shaved head and said, "Now is not the time." And then he disappeared. Literally, before my eyes.

I just stood there for a second. I mean, what would you do? Myself, I blew out a big breath of air and cursed.

"Lucernis," I muttered to myself as I made my way up to the hill he'd indicated, "gets weirder every damned day."

I was a little late. They'd already had the ceremonial meal and were cleaning up from that. Which was fine; as much as I cared for Corbin, he wasn't smelling like a flower, and despite the careful makeup he looked like what he was- a corpse propped up in a comfy chair at the head of the funerary table. It reminded me of nothing so much as some sort of gruesome child's tea party, but like I said, I'm not from Lucernis. Where I come from, somebody dies, you bury them if you have some land or burn them if you don't. You say a few words, and then get back to the business of living and grieving. Or celebrating, as the case may be.

Osskil sat on his brother's right, and three other men I didn't know took up the other seats, except for the one at the foot of the table. The one reserved for spouses or significant others. That one was empty. I wondered if Estra knew of the funeral, or if she'd simply chosen not to come.

The men were all of advanced age, with impressive facial hair. They looked so alike they had to be brothers. They were dressed in finery that looked just a tad threadbare. Professional mourners, I supposed. The other noble houses weren't going to be sending representatives; Corbin was an embarrassment. They'd all just politely ignore the whole thing.

Osskil rose and bowed when he saw me, but addressed himself to Corbin.

"Your friend Amra has come, Corbin. I told you she would. She's a bit late for the meal, but perhaps we can persuade her to have a drink with us?" The other men nodded and smiled encouragement.

"A drink would be very welcome," I managed, and Osskil made a bottle appear and filled glasses for everyone, including Corbin of course.

"Perhaps we could persuade Amra to give us a toast, Corbin?"

"Oh, I don't think—"

"A toast! A toast!" The other men quickly started up, and Osskil gave me a look that said, 'Give the dead man a toast, you mannerless savage.' And so I did.

I raised my glass, cleared my throat, and said "Corbin knew—" A glare from Osskil. "—that is to say, Corbin, you *know* that I am not one for public speaking. You, ah, are a good man. I am lucky to count you as my friend."

A chorus of 'Hear her! Hear her!' from the others. I had no idea what else to say. I cast a desperate glance at Osskil and he nodded and put back his drink, so I did as well, expecting wine.

It looked like wine, and tasted like wine for the most part, but there was something else to it and my head almost immediately began to spin and my heart started thumping up in my ears. I looked at Osskil again and he tilted his head toward his brother.

Corbin sat, grinning, at the head of the table. He was looking straight at me, and I knew that grin. It was one he reserved for the petty, hilarious misfortunes of others. No malice in it, just good humor. Then he looked over at his brother, and his face sobered. He raised his glass to Osskil and nodded, and Osskil did the same.

And then the world rushed back in, and Corbin was just a corpse once more. But his cup had tumbled to the grass. Empty.

"Well. That was... unexpected." I managed. Seeing Corbin apparently returned to life, even if only briefly, had touched a nerve. It was an unlooked-for gift, but it also brought back the rawness of his loss. I wasn't sure if the trade-off was worth it.

"A special wine, in a special place, for a special man," said one of the mourners. Osskil said nothing. The redness of his eyes spoke for him.

Then it was time to bundle him up and stick him in his tomb. They just lifted him, chair and all, and walked him into the mausoleum. Put him in a patch of light from a stained-glass window. Put a delicate little wrought-iron table next to him, and loaded it up with food and drink. And that was that. Or so I thought.

Osskil was the last one out. I heard him whisper 'Farewell, little brother' and saw him kiss the top of Corbin's head. Then he came out and closed the door.

The thief in me wondered where the lock was, and said so out loud.

"What need for locks in the City of the Dead? The dead know their own, Amra, as you have seen. You are welcome here, for Corbin has acknowledged you. And if an interloper were to dare disturb his rest, well, that's what the Guardian is for."

"The Guardian? I thought that was just some kind of granny tale to keep the kids out of the graveyard."

"Most assuredly not. The Guardian of the Dead is as real as you are, and ancient, and hideously powerful. The strictures posted at the gate are there to keep us living safe from it."

"Even the one about hurdy-gurdy music?"

He smiled. "Perhaps not that one. I suspect it's there just to preserve a sense of class."

"So blood, fornicating and littering all make the Guardian upset, eh?"

"Absolutely. Especially blood. Never, ever spill blood here, Amra. The Guardian *will* notice, and investigate. You don't want to meet it."

"No offense, Lord Osskil, but I'm just the slightest bit sceptical."

"Look over there. You see that mausoleum, the one with the gargoyles doing unspeakable things to each other? That's the final resting place of Borkin Breaves."

"The richest man in Lucernis?"

"Indeed he was. Still is. Inside his crypt I know for a fact are sacks and sacks of gold and jewels. I was at the funeral when they carted it all in. I was just a boy, then."

"You do realize who you're talking to, right?"

He gave me a sober look. "Please don't think about trying to rob Breaves' crypt, Amra."

"Why the hells not?"

"Besides the fact that it is incredibly gauche to rob the dead, you mean? Because when Breaves was put into his tomb, there were no gargoyles adorning the edifice. No adornment of any sort, in fact. It was just a big, ugly, plain marble cube. People were scandalized."

"Oh, please," I said. "You're saying the Guardian transformed those who tried to rob the tomb into that?"

"The Guardian has a vile sense of humor. Go and take a look. I know you won't take my word for it."

"Absolutely."

The other men had packed up all the funeral oddments and were waiting for Osskil.

"Farewell, Amra. Thank you for coming. It meant much to Corbin."

"It meant a lot to me as well." I stuck out my hand and he shook it, then held onto it for an extra beat.

"Call upon me when you are ready to move on Corbin's murderer. Please."

"All right."

He moved off down the hill with his group of rented mourners, and I ambled over to Borkin Breaves's tomb. The gargoyles were indeed doing things to each other, and by the looks on their disturbingly human faces, nobody was having much fun with it. Didn't prove anything, of course. I didn't believe a word of it. But then I doubted there was even a single gold mark in the mausoleum, either.

There was one gargoyle down low, half-obscured by weeds. Something about it made me take a second look. I pushed back the milky stalks and stared right into the scream-frozen face of Tolum Handy.

Tolum Handy was a thief who worked with Daruvner, same as me.

He'd disappeared the year before.

CHAPTER 17

It was well past midnight when Holgren and I arrived at the Cock's Spur. I'd pulled Holgren away from his 'meditation'—which to me looked suspiciously like a nap. Unless his whistling snore was a magely chant of sorts. If so, Bone's rumbling, snuffling snore was the perfect counterpoint.

I told him what I intended to do, and what Daruvner had made me promise. Holgren had agreed with Daruvner, in a bleary-eyed, grumpy sort of way.

I'd made one stop on our way to the Rookery, at Temple Street, north of Temple Market. At the modest temple of Bath the Silent, to be more precise. God of secrets.

Unlike its grand neighbors, there was no scrollwork, no fluted columns, no larger-than-life statuary to grace the front of Bath's temple, no maxims carved into stone and picked out in gold-leaf. His temple was built from porphyry, speckled gray and white, where others were faced with white marble or alabaster. And it was a small place, as these things go.

It was where people went to unburden their souls, secure in the knowledge someone would listen, and never tell. Holgren waited outside, insisting his secrets were his own and that he intended to keep it that way. I shrugged and climbed the well-worn steps to the small, unassuming nave.

A lesser-known aspect of Bath was that he didn't just receive confessions. He, or rather his priests, also held on to valuables. Anything that could be considered a secret was safe with the Silent One.

This was where I kept my retirement money. It earned no interest as it would with a money lender, but it also incurred no fees, and it was as safe in Bath's Temple as it would be anywhere in the world. I certainly wouldn't try to steal from him. What happened to the bodies of those who *had* tried was a secret, too.

An acolyte met me at the narrow door, quite nondescript except for the fact that his lips had been sewn shut. I'd always wondered how they ate. Another of Bath's secrets, I suppose. He led me through silent halls bathed in soft candlelight and faintly scented with some unfamiliar, musky incense. I had come to think of that scent as the smell of secrets, and for all I know that's exactly what it was.

The place was bigger inside, somehow, than it appeared to be from the street. How much bigger I didn't know, but big enough to make me believe Bath had potent magics at his disposal.

A short time later we stopped at a plain oak door, and the acolyte ushered me through. Inside was a small, bare white room. The only furniture was a small table, on which rested eleven chains: Long, narrow bars of buttery gold cast to break precisely into ten even pieces, or staves. Ten marks to a stave. Ten staves to a chain. Eleven hundred gold marks. Which left me with about a half-dozen marks to my name once I hauled them to the Rookery.

No secrets from Bath.

I loaded the chains into a satchel I'd brought along for the purpose, and turned to go. I was surprised to find the acolyte still standing in the doorway.

"My master has a message for you."

The little hairs on the back of my neck shot up, half because of the magic that had flooded the room, half because him talking to me was very, very creepy. It had certainly never happened before.

"How do you do that with your lips sewn shut?"

He smiled, which was rather ghastly to look at. "I can't tell you. I could show you...?"

"Um. No, thanks. What message does the high priest have for me?"

He shook his head. "Not Dalthas."

"Oh. You mean—" The goose bumps were crawling, now. I shivered despite myself.

"Yes."

Bath himself had a message for me? What the hells?

"My Master bids me tell you to beware She Who Casts Eight Shadows."

"Who might that be?" But I remembered the bloodwitch's warning about the Eightfold Bitch, and her Blade.

"My master does not say."

"I'm surprised he said anything. Being the Silent and all."

The acolyte smiled that horrid little smile again. "Secrets are my master's coin. And while he is frugal, he is not a miser. He spends carefully, but that is not the same as hoarding."

"So, not Bath the Silent. What then? Bath the Very Quiet? Bath the Extremely Reticent?"

"As you like. But now you too have a secret, of sorts. You would be wise to keep it."

"Is that a warning from your master?"

"Advice from my lowly self. Those who come here to admit faults, failings, sins... well, would they come if they knew the Silent One sometimes spoke?"

I shrugged. "Bath chose to share a secret with me. I think I can stand to keep a secret about him."

He bowed his head and drifted out the door. I followed, and met Holgren on the steps. As we walked towards the Rookery, I asked him "Have you ever heard of somebody called She Who Casts Eight Shadows?"

"A goddess. Killed during the Wars of the Gods. Why?"

"I don't know. I'm supposed to beware her, apparently. But if she's dead—Did you say *wars*, as in more than one?"

"Oh yes. There were several leading up to the last. Everyone tends to focus on the last one. But what's this about bewaring a goddess?"

I smiled. "It's a secret. If you'd come in with me...."

He arched one eyebrow and frowned. And let the matter drop.

~ ~ ~

The Rookery after midnight was unpleasant. Human wreckage littered the gutters, sometimes indistinguishable from all the garbage until a head moved or a hand was held out in mute appeal. I'd forgotten how depressing the Rookery was, along with how awful the stench could be in summer.

The darkened streets fairly seethed with bad intent, along with misery and abject poverty. Bravos loitered in front of taverns and shuttered shops, passing bottles of piss ale and laughing too loudly for genuine humor. Eyes tracked us as we walked to the front of the Cock's Spur, weighed us, judged whether we were predators or prey. Or maybe that was too easy a conceit. Everyone was meat here. It was just a question of how tough the meat might be, whether it was worth the bother of bringing it down and chewing it up.

"The big fish eat the little fish," Holgren murmured, echoing my thoughts in a way, "Except, I suppose, when the little fish band together to eat the big fish."

I grunted. If these surroundings made Holgren philosophical it shouldn't have surprised me. He chose to live next to the charnel grounds, after all. For myself, it just reminded me of the bad old days. Bellarius. Another city, another time, even another life, it sometimes seemed to me. But not long enough ago and not far enough away, and if I happened to forget, I needed only to look at my own scarred face reflected in a mirror, or a stranger's eyes.

I took in the leaning, ramshackle two-story building in front of us. It was all of wood, and rotting. It hadn't seen paint in a generation. The termites probably had to hold hands to keep it standing.

"Do termites have hands?" I asked Holgren.

"I doubt it. I've never checked. Why?"

"Come on," I said, "let's get this done. The sooner we're out of here, the better." And I walked in through the slightly skewed door of the Cock's Spur, Holgren at my heels.

In a place like the Cock's Spur, they don't even bother putting out chairs or benches that don't face the door. Nobody wants their back to any trouble that enters. As I came through the door, a couple dozen pairs of eyes skewered me. Well, except for the one hairy brute that had lost a beady, pig-like peeper somewhere, and in the not-too distant past, judging from the pus weeping out of the socket. He really should have considered an eye patch; if not for himself, then at least for anyone forced to look at him.

After a heartbeat, all the eyes slid right off me onto Holgren, which gave me faith in the fetish he'd given me. Or maybe it was the quality of his clothes. I heard Holgren sniff behind me.

"What's that smell?" he murmured.

"I think they're brewing ale."

"Oh. I thought it was cat urine. Is it supposed to smell that way?"

"Maybe the house recipe calls for cat piss." I'd heard of stranger ingredients, if not less disgusting. Bludgeoned roosters and the like. There was a reason I generally stuck to wine.

"I find myself appallingly unthirsty," said Holgren.

"Come on, let's brace the bartender."

"About the ingredients?"

"About the owner."

"Good idea. Take your complaint to the top, I always say." Holgren was nervous. He joked when he was nervous, I'd finally figured out. That Holgren was nervous made me nervous. Which made me pissy. I strode over to the bar along the left-hand wall where the tap man was pushing a filthy rag along the filthy bar top.

"When you're done rearranging the dirt, I want to speak to Gavon."

"Ee innt ear," the spindly man said, or something like it.

"Sorry, could you speak a human language?"

He hawked and spat. "Gavon's not 'ere."

I lifted the heavy satchel to the bar top and lifted the flap so he could see. "Get him here, and soon, or I'll let everybody in the place have a look at this. If I do that, they'll try to take it away from me, and then me and my friend will have to kill them all. That won't be good for business."

He stared at me for a second. "You couldn't take um all."

"If they take Gavon's gold, it won't matter if we could or couldn't. Not to you, anyway, because he'll kill you for pissing around instead of minding his business."

He thought about that. "That's a point. Stay 'ere."

He drifted up a set of decrepit stairs into the gloom above. Three of the bigger patrons seemed to take that as a signal of opportunity. They got up and walked toward Holgren and me, bad intent written all over their faces. I slipped a knife into the palm of my hand, but Holgren stepped between me and them.

"Gentlemen," he said, purple light suddenly arcing from hand to hand, "the tap man will be back shortly. I'm sure he'll see to refills then. Until such time, I suggest you remain seated."

Two of them saw the sense in that. One, a lean man with enormous hands, fingered something under his shirt. Some sort of talisman. I could see him deciding to place his faith in it.

"Why, I just wanted to have a word, all private-like," he said. "You being newcomers to this fine establishment and all, I thought—" and the knife came from his waist and towards Holgren's throat in a blur of reflected lantern light.

Holgren was quick, quicker than I would have given him credit for. He twisted away, and the knife blade kissed his earlobe on its way to being buried in the wall behind the bar.

The man wasn't waiting to see if his blade would do the job; he was already rushing in with those big hands clenched into fists. Holgren put his own hand out, palm forward, and that purple arcing light leaped from his hand to the would-be killer's face. Where it began to gnaw at the flesh like a hungry animal. In an instant I could see the man's teeth through a hole in his cheek. He screamed and stumbled, and clawed at his own face. He fell to the hard-packed dirt floor and screamed some more. Holgren fingered his cut earlobe. His hand came away red. He pulled a handkerchief out of his sleeve.

"That's enough, mage." A voice from the stairs, mild, a little high pitched. I glanced up and saw a supremely nondescript man drumming his fingers against the railing, the tap man behind him.

"He started it, Gavon."

"So finish it, Angrado."

"Fine." Holgren did nothing that I could see, but the weird light playing on what was left of the man's face winked out. The man stopped screaming after a few seconds. I glanced at him, then took a double take. The only wounds on his face were the claw marks he'd made himself.

Holgren leaned down, elbows on knees, and said conversationally, "That trinket around your neck has never been within a mile of a mage. Until tonight." Then he stood and walked toward the stairs. After a moment, I followed.

CHAPTER 18

"**W**hy didn't you kill him, Angrado?" Gavon asked as he motioned us to sit at a candlelit table in the center of the upstairs gloom.

"Why should I bother?" Holgren replied.

Gavon chuckled. "You always were too squeamish for your own good. That one won't thank you for sparing him. He'll kill you if he can."

"But he can't. Not on his best day. And if I'm squeamish, what does that make you?"

"A man unconcerned with niceties."

"You mean morals. Or is it scruples?"

Gavon smiled, mirthlessly. "No one can hold a grudge like a Low Countryman, it seems."

"You would know, wouldn't you? But I'm only half Low Country, as you seemed to take every opportunity to point out."

"I believe I also said you were half a man."

Holgren grinned, and I knew things were about to turn ugly. "Mariette seemed to think I was man enough," he said. "How *is* your sister?"

And that's when the knives came out. Gavon suddenly held two huge pig stickers, and Holgren a spitting, hissing blade of white light. They were both standing, chairs knocked back.

"I'll see your half-breed guts on the floor for that," said Gavon. Holgren just smiled.

I cleared my throat. "So I guess you two know each other?"

"Oh, yes," said Gavon. "Holgren Angrado and I have a history."

I turned to look at Holgren. "You might have mentioned that," I said.

"You never asked."

"I have an idea," I said. "Let's put away the blades and do some business. Gavon, you can still kill somebody, and make a profit to boot." I heaved the satchel up onto the table in front of him. His eyes flickered to all that gold. His knives disappeared and suddenly he was smiling. He deliberately turned away from Holgren to face me directly.

"Knowing that one won't get you a discount, you know. In fact, I should charge extra."

"Believe me, I am regretting his acquaintance at the moment." Holgren took the hint and extinguished his blade.

"So talk to me."

I heaved an inner sigh of relief. Outwardly, I put on my dubious face. "To be honest, I don't think you'll touch this contract."

"I have never yet come across one that couldn't be fulfilled."

"I'd want you to execute it personally."

"Now that is a problem. I don't really do that anymore. Only on special occasions, you might say."

"Well then, I'm sorry to have wasted your time." I flipped the satchel closed and began to heave it back on my shoulder.

"Let's hear it, at least," said Gavon, taking his seat again.

I took off Holgren's fetish. "You inked a contract on one Amra Thetys. I want to take out a contract on anyone who turns up to get paid for it."

He laughed outright. "Oh, you've got balls, I'll give you that. It's almost clever. I suppose you'd want it to be public knowledge, as well."

"Naturally. The dead don't care about revenge."

"What made you think I would agree to something like this?"

I put on a puzzled expression. "Money, of course. One chain just for saying yes, and ten more on the off chance you have to kill someone."

"I could kill you right now, earn the original contract, and take what you brought."

"That's what he's here for." I jabbed a thumb in Holgren's direction. "Besides, you wouldn't. Bad for your reputation, killing prospective clients."

Gavon sat back, drumming his fingers on the arm of his chair. "If I agree, I'll open myself up to all kinds of headaches. People trying to outbid contracts. It will be a mess."

"Yes. I can see it escalating, people trying to outbid each other. And every one of them paying a ten per cent, non-refundable commission to you. All that gold piling up will be very messy indeed."

Slowly, he smiled. "I do like the way you think. But unfortunately, I can't personally take this commission. I have to maintain my impartiality." He leaned forward. "I'll ink the contract, and I'll spread the word, and you will just have to take your chances that it's enough. And if the original client wishes to up their offer, well..." He shrugged.

"I suppose that will have to do." It wasn't everything I had hoped for, but I thought it would be enough. For a while, at least. I stood, and he followed suit.

"I'll be wanting my ten chains back soon, Gavon. Once I kill your other client."

"We'll see."

"I know who it is, but confirmation would be nice. You wouldn't want to help me with that, would you?"

"I'm afraid I have to keep that confidential, being part of the service and all. It's been a pleasure, Amra Thetys. May I suggest you leave through the back? I imagine there are a half-dozen cutthroats waiting for you in front by now. News travels fast in the Rookery when the news is gold-colored. Holgren, of course, is welcome to leave the way he came."

~ ~ ~

News indeed travelled fast, but Holgren blew through the motley collection of murderers waiting for us outside like an autumn storm off the Dragonsea. Quite literally. It's hard to stick a knife in someone when you're rolling down the street, being pushed along by gale-force winds. Holgren was proving to be a lot more powerful—and versatile—than I'd ever imagined. And I have an active imagination.

We made it back to civilization in time for last call at Tambor's. Holgren bought a jug, owing to the fact that I was now virtually destitute, and we sat outside at one of the scarred tables and sipped vinegar. After a silent while Holgren finally spoke up.

"You know what you've done, don't you?"

"Um, saved my own neck?"

"Yes, that. Probably. But you've also changed the face of low justice in Lucernis forever." He shook his head. "Gavon has been running the murder-for-hire racket in Lucernis for nearly a decade. Given twice as long, he never would have thought of your ploy. You've made that bastard richer than he ever dreamed, in one night."

"So you did know we were going to see him! Why didn't you tell me you knew him?"

He smiled. "As I said, you never asked. To be honest, I was hoping things would get out of hand so I could kill him."

"What is it between you two?"

"We grew up together, in Fel-Radoth. He is my cousin, once removed. We were never what you would call friendly."

"He's got to be twenty years older than you."

"One of the advantages of being a mage, Amra, is that you don't have to look your age."

"Did you really sleep with his sister?"

He shuddered. "Mariette? I'd sooner sleep with a pheckla. Certainly less dangerous, and probably more pleasurable. Guache was considered the nice one of the brood." He shifted his gaze from the bowl of wine in front of him to the street running beside Tambor's arbor, where we sat.

I don't remember what I was going to say next, because suddenly Holgren was lunging over the table at me, knocking me down to the ground. I do remember getting a hand around a knife hilt, and then the world erupting in flame.

"Stay low!" Holgren hissed, then rolled off me and sat up. He made an intricate gesture with one hand, face grim as death, and suddenly the flames vanished, leaving charred, smoking ruins around us that, seconds before, had been Tambor's arbor. And some of Tambor's other customers.

In the street, people were screaming and running. A dray horse bolted in its traces, and in its fear reduced the cart and its driver to pulp. The immediate surroundings were complete chaos, but the chaos was fleeing the vicinity as fast as it could, leaving a stillness in its wake.

I heard clapping. I looked out into the street and saw Bosch walking toward us, half a dozen swordsmen at his back. He was clapping in time with his own dragging footsteps.

"Excellent negation," he said, "especially *extempore*. I applaud you, sir."

Holgren stood up and brushed himself off. "I am going to kill you for that," he said mildly, and sauntered out into the street towards Bosch.

"Please, let's avoid unnecessary confrontation. For my part, I apologize," said Bosch. "I had no idea a fellow magus would be in the thief's company. I will happily make amends. As soon as I secure her corpse." He pointed his stubbled chin towards me. "What do you say?"

"I say you talk too much."

"So be it," said Bosch, and another inferno burst forth from his open hands, engulfing Holgren in a maelstrom of flame. I could barely make out his form, a dark, wavering blur at the heart of a torrent of fire. I saw his smudged silhouette crumple. I saw Bosch grin, beads of sweat rolling down his face, dripping from his nose and unshaven chin. The men with him stood watching, most with mouths agape. A mage's duel isn't something you see every day.

Finally, the river of fire sputtered, slowed to a trickle, failed. It was eerily silent.

Holgren was down on one knee. His clothes smoked, but his lean face was cold.

"My turn," he said, and flicked the fingers of one hand.

Bosch's body literally exploded, splattering his swordsmen and twenty yards of the cobbled street with blood and bloody gobbets of flesh. All that was left of him was his head, which fell to the ground and, I swear to Kerf, blinked for a few seconds. My stomach did a backflip at that.

"You'd best be on your way," said Holgren to the sell-swords, and they saw the sense in that. Holgren picked up Bosch's head by its lank, greasy hair. Stared into the shocked, blinking eyes.

Bosch mouthed a word and his eyes went cold and dead. Nobody home.

"Bloody hells," Holgren spat. He looked at me, and there was something feral in his eyes. "He's jumped."

"What? What does that mean?"

"It means we haven't seen the last of him. He'll be back, in some form or fashion. That's a trick you can only get by treating with infernal powers. Bosch" Holgren said with plain distaste, "is a daemonist. Let's go."

I nodded. The watch couldn't be far away. We needed to leave. "Go where?"

"Back to Gavon's. Where else?"

"But if Bosch isn't really dead—"

"He is. It's just that he's bought himself a short encore. Do you want the contract on you cancelled or not?"

"By all means, let's go see your cousin."

We set off down the nearest alley. We stopped only once, while I stole somebody's freshly laundered shirt from a second story drying pole. Holgren took it from me without a word and wrapped Bosch's noggin in it, using the tag-ends of the sleeves as a handle.

You can't just go walking around with a severed head in Lucernis. But you can, I discovered, walk around with a lumpy head-shaped item, wrapped in linen and dripping blood. I think it's just that nobody really wants to know you're walking around with a severed head, and are appreciative of the courtesy of leaving room for doubt.

In any case, nobody gave us more than a second glance, and the second-glancers made sure to move along quickly, giving us a wide berth.

Whatever Holgren was feeling, he kept it bottled up. I stole the occasional glance at him as we walked, and the best I can say was his face had gone from cold to stony. As for me, I was coming to terms with what I'd seen him do.

I have seen and caused death. It's never pretty. There is no 'right' way to kill — if you need to kill somebody, you do it any way that works. It wasn't the fact that Holgren had been so cold about turning Bosch into a red smear, and it wasn't that Bosch had met such a spectacularly disgusting demise. What bothered me was just how easily Holgren had done it. He'd decided Bosch was going to die, and just like that, Bosch was dead. Messily, spectacularly, violently dead.

That kind of raw power was terrifying.

It seemed impossible that I'd been joking with someone who could, just by wiggling his fingers, turn me into a fine red mist.

So. There was a certain reserve that sprang up between us on that walk.

When we arrived at the Cock's Spur for the second time that night, Holgren didn't make any jokes, and nobody else felt like trying their luck.

CHAPTER 19

olgren just sort of blasted the door off its hinges and strolled in, swinging Bosch's head back and forth in a bored, idle way. The scum and villainy that was the Cock's Spur's patrons wisely remained seated and avoided eye contact. Holgren climbed the splintered wooden stairs to Guache's office. I followed.

Holgren blasted the office door, too.

Guache was sitting at his table, eating a very late dinner. Pork pie, from the smell. My satchel full of gold was still in front of him. He didn't look up, didn't say anything, didn't acknowledge Holgren in any way. He just went about shovelling pork pie into his mouth like he hadn't a care in the world. When Holgren tossed Bosch's wrapped head onto the table, Guache finally glanced at him, and that glance was pure contempt.

These two men truly hated each other, and one of them would kill the other, and probably sooner rather than later. That much I felt in my gut.

"You sent word to Bosch as soon as we left," I said.

"Before that, actually," replied Guache.

"Well there's his head."

Guache leaned back in his chair, wiped his mouth with one sleeve. "I had a cat that used to bring me dead things too. Are you applying to be my pet, Amra Thetys?"

Holgren cursed and slammed Guache out of his chair with one fist. Guache was up again in an instant, knives out, and Holgren murmured some harsh syllable and suddenly Guache Gavon was spread-eagled against the wall. His feet did not touch the ground. Strain as he might, Guache Gavon was pinned to the wall, utterly helpless and in thrall to Holgren's magic. He looked bored.

"I've brought you Bosch's head, Gavon. Now my partner is taking her ten chains back."

Gavon opened his mouth to say something, but whatever it was, was lost as a little black nightmare exploded through the window shutters.

All teeth and claws, and reeking of rotting blood and charred flesh, it was a little smaller than Bone. It smashed through the wooden slats as though they were made of paper and landed on the table, hissing and lashing a barbed tail. It had the head of a boyne beetle. If boyne beetles grew to dog size.

Holgren dropped his cousin and started another spell.

Too late. The thing snatched up Bosch's head and was out the window again before he had got two liquid syllables past his lips. I'm embarrassed to say I didn't even get a knife out until it was gone.

"By all the dead gods, what was that?" I said.

"Daemonette." Holgren spat. "We definitely haven't seen the last of that foul daemonist."

Gavon started laughing. Genuine, humor-filled laughter. I swear, tears started in the corners of his eyes. After a few seconds it seemed he was having trouble catching his breath.

"Looks like I'll be holding onto your gold for a while longer," he finally managed, then started up laughing again.

Gavon was still chuckling as we left. His mirth followed us down the stairs and out the door.

~ ~ ~

False dawn was scratching at the sky by the time Holgren and I made it back to his sanctum. He wasn't in much of a talking mood. He flopped down on his dusty couch and Bone sauntered over to him and put his heavy head in Holgren's lap. Holgren rubbed it idly and stared off into nothing.

"We know Bosch was—is—working for this Elamner, besides being friendly with creatures from hells," I said. "It only stands to reason that his boss is the one behind everything. Corbin's death. The contract on my life. The only problem is, I think the Elamner might actually be dead."

"What do you mean?"

"That's right. I never told you about breaking into his villa." I told Holgren about the corpse I'd seen, the knife sticking out of his chest, the magic that had infused the room.

Holgren gave me a flat stare. "Just to make sure, you are aware that I'm a mage, correct?"

"I know sarcasm fits you like a tailored suit, but I'm a little tired. Can you get to the point?"

"What you saw wasn't a murder scene, ritual or otherwise. It was a containment ritual. A brutal one, from the Ardesh steppes. The man you saw wasn't dead. He was just... paused."

"Paused? What the hells does that mean?"

"Paused. Suspended. Taken out of time. Put on ice. Take the knife out of his heart, and his life resumes. It's a rather tricky bit of magic. You've got to slip the knife in precisely between heartbeats."

"Shit. So Bosch really is just a flunky for the Elamner?"

He shrugged. "I don't know how you come to that conclusion. Just because he didn't murder his employer doesn't mean he hasn't gone rogue. Or don't you think a daemonist would be capable of lying to, cheating on or stealing from his employer?"

I waved that away. "No, listen. This Elamner, Heirus, hires a mage, gets him to perform this ritual. It sure as hells didn't look like something you could surprise somebody with."

"No. It would require willing participation."

"What sort of person would want to be taken out of life like that? Suspended?"

"I haven't the faintest idea."

"I do. Somebody who doesn't have much time left. Someone who needs to ration it. Somebody who is sick, maybe. Dying. Maybe in constant pain. Somebody waiting for a Kerf-damned cure."

Holgren smiled. "Oh, you are clever, Amra. Perhaps a cure from the Age of the Gods?"

I stood up and walked to the door. "Don't melt that toad down yet, Holgren. I think we need to know a little more before we do anything that can't be undone."

"Probably wise. Where are you going?"

"There's a nobleman I need to visit on the Promenade."

"I should probably say something amusing, but all that comes to mind is 'huh?'"

"It's Corbin's long-lost brother. If we're going to make a social call on the Elamner, we're going to need some hired blades. I haven't got any more money, but Baron Thracen does. And he's got a good reason to spend it."

"If you have time, perhaps you could visit Lagna's temple as well and see if that old man knows anything about the toad."

I groaned.

"What?"

"I don't like him. He's smelly and makes me feel like an idiot."

"He makes everyone feel like an idiot. He's the high priest of the god of knowledge."

"Fine. But you're going to have to lend me some money for his fee."

"It's not a fee. It's an offering."

I snorted.

"Anything you'd like me to do?" he asked, passing me a few marks.

I stopped. "Actually, yes." I fished Bosch's hair from the button I'd wound it around, handed it to him. "Do you think you can find Bosch with this, even though he hasn't got a body anymore?"

He took it and smiled. It wasn't a friendly smile. "Oh, certainly."

"If Baron Thracen agrees to help us, I'll have him send a runner to you. I want to move tonight. Or even earlier."

"That sounds suspiciously like a plan."

"No, it sounds like a steaming hot mess. We'll see if it improves."

CHAPTER 20

Osskil wasn't home.

The gate guard at the Thracen manse didn't want to tell me even that much until I gave my name, then after a muttered conference with his partner who then disappeared inside, someone higher up the servants' ladder came out and informed me that the baron was breakfasting with Lord Morno, and would be pleased to see me in the early afternoon. I guess Osskil had left instructions.

I was a little surprised that Osskil was important enough to be having meals with Morno. Lord Morno, the governor of Lucernis, generally has his hands full, what with all the political manoeuvring that comes with ruling the largest city in the West. Morno's a law and order man to his black, shrivelled soul. Governing Lucernis must be enough to make him dyspeptic. I doubt he gets much sleep.

For decades, the hereditary rulers of Lucernis were so inept and bumbling or corrupt and cruel that the king finally had to eradicate their line and appoint a governor. Morno was unlucky enough to be competent and loyal and, rumor has it, one of the queen's favorites. King Vos III is no idiot. With a queen twenty years his junior, Morno was handed the high honor of restoring the rule of law to Lucernis, which just happens to be some four hundred miles from court. Was Morno her lover? Who knows? But he's been taking it out on the city ever since.

Pirates no longer linger just off shore, and riots are a rare thing nowadays; fewer starve and many even pay at least token taxes. Morno keeps the largest city on the Dragonsea from coming apart at the seams.

Doesn't mean I like the bastard.

With a few hours to kill, I set off for Temple Street to talk to the grumpiest, most knowledgeable person in Lucernis.

~ ~ ~

"I'm old and I'm tired and it's time for my nap. Go away."

He was the high priest of Lagna, god of knowledge. Which meant he was a jumped-up librarian, since Lagna happened to be dead.

Lagna's temple was big, with big glassed windows and a huge main room, or chapel, or whatever it was called, but it had seen better days. It hadn't seen a good cleaning in decades, most probably. Offerings, it seemed, were scarce. Maybe that was because people didn't value knowledge as much as they should. Or maybe it was because Lhiewyn, the high priest, was an extremely grumpy bastard with a tongue sharper than any of my knives.

I couldn't argue that he was old; his wrinkles had wrinkles and his hair was little more than a silver net across his spotted pate. He leaned on a crooked cane, and one leg looked like it was just so much dead weight. The young acolyte who had directed me to his cell in back of the book-crammed temple was probably as much a servant to the old man as he was to Lagna.

"I need your help, priest."

"That you need help is bleeding obvious," he said, taking in my appearance. "I doubt there's any help for you, though."

"How much for a little information on pre-Diaspora artefacts, specifically golden toad statuettes stashed away in ancient temples in the swamps of Gol-Shen?"

"Oh, that won't cost you anything, because I know piss-all about them. I serve the god of knowledge, not trivia. You nitwit. Jessep, show this bald, brainless twit out."

Gods, but I hated talking to this old codger. Sometimes I had to, though, when I took a more esoteric contract. It was never much fun.

"What about a goddess who casts eight shadows? Also likes knives or blades or some such?"

His eyebrows rose. "You want to know about the Eightfold Goddess?"

"No. I thought I'd ask just so you could feel superior some more."

"Now there is an interesting deity. Very few know about her, actually. Or rather, that her eight aspects are just that, and not—"

"So I've found one of your favorite topics. That's great. I've actually got somewhere to be today, though." All right, that wasn't particularly fair. I'd brought it up. But he looked like he was settling in for a long, long monologue.

"Well, then, we should start with those weapons you mentioned. I bet you like to stab things, so this should hold your miniscule attention." He sat down carefully on a three-legged stool that stood next to his pallet. They were the only furnishings in the room, so I stood. He heaved a pained sigh and straightened his dead leg out before him. Jessep stood in the corner and tried to hide a smirk.

"Some say She fashioned Her Blades from bits of the other gods," he said, "from gobbets of immortal flesh and bone that lay scattered about the battlefields of the Divine during the Age of Chaos. Thus is truth distorted over millennia.

"The truth is She was taken by Shem, Low Duke of the Eleven Hells. Her father sold Her to Shem, to be his handmaid. That one tried to rape Her eight times, but each time She left a piece of Herself behind for him to sate his lust on. Seven times he was not sated, but on the eighth his strength was spent along with his seed. And then the One Who Is Eight tore Shem to pieces with eight pairs of hands. They say that She made the Blades from his horns, his bones, his scales and claws and fangs.

"She is terrible, and beautiful, and no god or demon fucks with Her, for She is as mad as they come and eight times as nasty."

"Are priests supposed to curse?"

His bushy eyebrows went up. "What, did I offend your delicate sensibilities? I'm too old to worry about what other people think."

"Why have I never heard of this goddess?"

"You mean besides being generally ignorant? Probably because there aren't many daft enough to worship Her. She might take notice. At best, some might say a prayer to one of Her Aspects. I hear the Fraternity of Blood, that band of assassins up in Pinghul, hold Kalara as their patron deity. They aver that Red Hand is her consort, which if you ask me is utter tripe. Anyway, She's supposed to be dead. Not that that ever means much where gods are concerned."

"Who is Kalara?"

"The Eight-fold Goddess has, try to imagine it, eight aspects. Kalara, Goddess of Assassins, is one. Let me see if I can remember all the others. Abanon, Goddess of hate. Moranos, deity of desire, Ninkashi, worker of retribution, Heletia, font of true sight and clarity. How many is that?"

"Five."

"Then there's Husth, goddess of deception and shadows. Very popular with thieves in Bellarius."

"I've actually heard of that one. But go on."

"Xith rules death and rebirth. And that leaves Visini, goddess of decay, inertia, chaos and despair. That's eight, right?"

"Yes."

"Mind you, together they make one. The Eight-fold Goddess."

"Which is all very interesting, but what about these blades?"

"I knew you'd like the stabby bit. I'll tell you what I know, but it isn't much. I'm a priest, not a weapon smith. Each one has some function pertaining to its particular aspect-Goddess. So Abanon's blade will use or feed on hate in some fashion, and Moranos's dagger will in some way be connected to desire. And so on."

I waited for him to continue, but apparently he was done. "That's it?" I asked.

"Well, in the presence of one, I'd rather be on the end that you hold. And given the choice I'd rather not be in the same country as any of them."

"Thanks so much for that useful bit of advice."

"They're the tools of an insane goddess, forged from the body of a demon lord. What did you expect? 'Weapon A can cut through armor as though it were butter, and weapon B lets you walk on water?'"

"Well, yes. Sort of. But I guess I see your point."

He shifted on his stool and his watery brown eyes got sort of glinty. "You came seeking information, but let me give you some advice. The world is still littered with artifacts left over from before the Cataclysm. *None* of them are safe to play with. I don't know why you want to know about the Eightfold's Blades, nor do I much care. But if by some mad chance you find one of Her Blades, or one finds you, remember one thing: Such tools *want* to be used, and to them, any mortal hand that wields them is a tool in turn. Be very, very careful. And leave your offering in the box in the foyer. Silver is good, gold is better. If you want more information you can go dig in the stacks. Jessep will help you since I very much doubt you can read. I've got to take my nap."

I turned to go. Turned back.

"One more question," I said. "A quick one."

He sighed, and gave me a long-suffering look.

"Is the Guardian of the Dead in the Necropolis real?"

"Of course it's real, you ignoramus. It's real, extremely nasty, and very unhappy with its job. I shudder to think what would happen if it ever escaped the Necropolis. Gods willing, it would stumble across you first. Now piss off."

I followed Jessep out to the stacks, which were just that—stacks and stacks of books, parchment, papyrus, scrolls and scraps. There was some sort of mad order to it, I could feel it in my bones, but it eluded me.

"So, Jessep, is there anything *not* unpleasant about that old codger?"

Jessep stopped to consider. He was a long time about it.

"Well, he makes a beef stew you'd slap your mother for," was all he eventually came up with.

Jessep did indeed help searching through the mad mess, and I did need him to read for me. What we eventually found was in a language that I'd never seen before. He'd found what I was looking for in a box of scrolls mouldy with age. Much good it did me.

On a scrap of papyrus that Jessep said was part of a chronicle of the War of the Gods was a prayer. Or a poem. Or maybe a prophecy. I'm not sure which, since the last bit was missing. Anyway, it listed the Goddesses' Blades by name. I had the youngster copy out a translation for me. Jessep was a damned good translator. He even made it rhyme:

> *Abanon wields the Blade that Whispers Hate,*
> *Moranos holds the Dagger of Desire,*
> *Ninkashi grips the trembling Blade of Rage,*
> *With which she pierced the heart of her mad sire.*

> *Heletia grips the Knife called Winter's Tooth,*
> *Visini wields the Blade that Binds and Blinds,*
> *Husth fights with the Kris that Strikes Elsewhere,*
> *And woe betide the soul it finally finds.*

> *Kalara hones the Knife that Parts the Night,*

Grim Xith commands the Dirk that Harrows Souls;
Eight blades the Goddess has, and one
From eight will ren—

And then the rest was so badly rat-gnawed that it was useless.

My gut told me I'd just picked up a piece of a puzzle. What puzzle, and where it fit, I had no idea.

CHAPTER 21

After a quick meal of bread and cheese and small beer in Temple Market, I walked back to the Promenade and the Thracen manse. I was tired. I couldn't remember the last time I slept. Was it in prison? Surely not.

This time I was let in like–well, not an honored guest, but at least not like I'd just stepped in something rotting. A servant in Thracen livery showed me to a small study, outfitted me with some wine, tried not to look like he wanted to warn me not to steal anything, and told me Osskil would see me soon. And he did.

Such a heavy man should have lumbered, but Corbin's brother entered the room like a coiled spring waiting to be released.

"Amra Thetys, you do me honor."

"I don't know about that, but I hope to do right by you today. I appreciate your help in Havelock."

He waved that away and sat down in a chair opposite mine. "Lord Morno wasn't pleased with me about that, but then Lord Morno is rarely pleased with anything. Tell me why you are here today," he said. And I did. About Bosch, the Elamner, and the villa. About the suppositions Holgren and I had come up with regarding the 'corpse' in the villa, and the golden toad.

"We should move soon," he said when I was done. "They might flee."

I liked him even better for automatically using *we* instead of *I*.

"Holgren and I hoped you'd feel that way. Do you think you could send someone to fetch him? He should be done working on the location spell for Bosch, and I guarantee you'll want him along when you call on the Elamner. Holgren's magic is very, uh, thorough," I said, thinking of the red ruin he'd made of Bosch's body.

"Certainly. I'll send a carriage round for him at once." He rang a bell and a servant appeared. I gave him directions for Holgren's hovel.

I was less pleased when Osskil also gave instructions to have Inspector Kluge invited over.

"You've got to be kidding," I said. "Kluge? He'll screw this up just so he can pin it on me and give me a hempen necklace."

"A necessary formality. Lord Morno can't be seen to countenance private justice among the nobles, as he made plain to me this morning. Kluge's inclusion gives our action the stamp of his authority. Don't worry, Amra. I'll impress upon the inspector just how dim a view the Thracens will take of it, should you be made to pay for assisting us."

"That's all well and good, but Courune is a long way from Lucernis, and you spanking Kluge will be cold comfort to me if I'm executed."

He smiled. "Have a little faith. Both Corbin and I learned early how to be persuasive. Now explain to me again the locations of the guards."

We went over the layout again in detail, making maps. Servants came and went. Things were whispered in Osskil's ear, and Osskil wrote notes and stamped them with the Thracen seal. The notes got carried off throughout the city by liveried servants.

By late afternoon, a small army had been assembled in Osskil's courtyard. Swordsmen, halberdiers and crossbowmen milled around, talking shop. There was even a pair of Westmarch arquebusiers off in a corner, polishing their big, bell-mouthed boom sticks. They must have been for show, because their weapons, while loud as Kerf's farts, weren't all that deadly unless you stuck your head in one.

"Seems a bit much," I told Osskil.

"You saw five armsmen total when you reconnoitred the surroundings the first and second times, but there might well be more. An unknown number may be guarding derelict villa and the interior of the manse proper. And no guardsman can be on duty all day and night, so it is best to prepare for double, if not treble the number we know of."

Holgren and Kluge arrived not long after that. Holgren exited the carriage, followed by Kluge. Holgren looked amused. Kluge looked like someone had pissed down his back and told him it was raining.

"How was your ride?" I asked Holgren, ignoring Kluge. He just smiled.

"Were you able to work up a locator spell for Bosch?"

"Yes, though I'm sorry to say it's not terribly accurate." He showed me an old brass compass, currently pointing west-southwest. Towards the villa. "I might have done better with more time, but not enough to make a real difference."

"I think it will be fine. It's more insurance than necessity anyway. Let me introduce you to Baron Thracen."

"Osskil, please," said the baron, shaking Holgren's hand. "It's a pleasure to meet you, Magister."

"Holgren, please," said Holgren, smiling. Looking around the courtyard, he said "I take it this will not be a stealthy operation? A platoon of warriors marching up the Jacos Road is a noticeable thing. I can attempt a glamour—"

"Oh, that won't be necessary. Amra has come up with a means for us to arrive at the villa's gates without drawing undue attention."

"Oh really?" said Holgren, raising an eyebrow at me.

"I'm not as much of an imbecile as Lagna's priest likes to make out," I replied. "You'll see."

"Holgren, Inspector Kluge, would you care to join me, Amra and Captain Ecini, my guard captain, in the study? Time flies, and we still have one stop to make in the Spindles before we call on this Elamner. I'd like to brief you on our plan of action and receive your comments."

They did, and the baron did. Holgren made a few remarks and assured us that he could and would neutralize the death curse on the Elamner's room before we entered the building. Kluge stood there like a post.

Twenty minutes later, just as night was falling, we were on our way to Alain's.

~ ~ ~

The look on Alain's face when I showed up at his yard at the head of a small army was priceless.

"We've had some complaints about the quality of your work," I said.

"Huh?"

I punched him in the arm. "Actually, we're here to borrow your optibus."

"Omnibus," he corrected automatically, taking in all the people with deadly things in their hands standing in the street outside his yard.

"Whatever. Can we borrow it?"

"Huh?"

Osskil stepped forward. "It's a pleasure to meet you, master Alain. I'd like to hire your omnibus for the evening, if that would be all right."

"It's not really mine, ser–"

"Baron Osskil det Thracen-Courune, at your service."

"My lord," said Alain, giving his forehead a knuckle. "But the omnibus isn't mine to lend."

"I assure you we will take care, and I will indemnify you and your client should anything happen to it. In addition to the rental fee, of course," Osskil reached into a belt pouch and brought out a fistful of gold.

"Of course," said Alain, taking the money in a sort of daze. He just sort of held it, as though he wasn't sure what to do with it. Myra came out from the shadows where she'd been observing the circus and took charge of the money, her husband and the situation. She gave me a questioning look and I shrugged and smiled.

She rounded up Alain's laborers, got the omnibus hitched and pointed towards the gate. Osskil had his personal coachman mount the box. The man looked half thrilled, half terrified. Our little private army climbed inside.

"Are we going to regret this?" Myra whispered to me.

"I really don't see how," I told her honestly, "but the night is still young." She tssked and got out of the way.

A crowd had gathered outside Alain's gate. Kluge walked out and said, "Go home." The small hairs on the back of my neck stirred when he said it. It wasn't a suggestion, or even a command; it was a Compulsion. The crowd broke up.

We were on our way.

CHAPTER 22

Half the men exited the omnibus at the same clearing where I'd stashed Kram on my first visit to the villa. They would work their way through the woods as quietly as they could and assault the house next to Heirus's, where at least three guards were stationed, when they heard the signal. Which was one of the arquebuses going off, preferably in somebody's face. They moved quickly and quietly out of sight, faster than the omnibus traveled.

By the time we arrived at Heirus's gate, they were to already be in position. If anything went wrong, they had a signaller as well—the other arquebusier.

The giant wagon rolled up to the gate, and kept going. I could see the curious looks of the gate guard through the small warped windows that punctuated the omnibus's side. It was only when the back end of the omnibus was roughly even with the gate that men with pointy things started boiling out, and the guard's expression changed from mild curiosity to fear. Once everybody else was out, I jumped off and followed. I didn't see what they did to turn the gate into twisted wreckage, but it wasn't the arquebus, because I saw—and heard—that one go off in clouds of foul smelling smoke. I didn't see if it injured anyone, but I rather doubted it.

The gate guard was sprawled on the ground in a spreading puddle of blood. Two other guards were running—not towards the villa, but to the abandoned estate next door, Osskil's troops in hot pursuit.

The two guards met several of their comrades, who were running *towards* the manse from the abandoned villa, with the other half of Osskil's private army on their heels. There had, apparently been considerably more than three armsmen stationed in the abandoned villa. That's when weapons started getting thrown to the ground and hands started grabbing sky, when it became apparent that they were being assaulted from two sides by superior numbers. All told, it was over in little more than a minute.

"Now the dangerous part begins," I told Osskil, while Heirus's sell-swords were bound and stuffed into the omnibus.

We left four men to guard the prisoners. Holgren and Kluge approached the front door the way you'd approach a tiger. The rest of us, Osskil, me and a dozen armsmen, waited behind them. There was a lot of muttering between the two, and some waving of hands, and then Holgren put his hand on the door. He stood there for a time, muttering something to himself in a language I didn't recognize. His hand began to glow. Finally, he turned to us.

"The wards are down, and the death curse negated. But this place is far from safe. When we go in, follow closely."

He pushed on the door, hand glowing, and it fell to the floor with a massive boom. A stench like rotting corpses billowed out of the unnaturally dark interior. He and Kluge walked over the fallen door and into the gloom, and the rest of us followed behind.

The walls were sort of melting; sagging and peeling away from the structure underneath, like decaying flesh sloughing off bones. I felt myself very much wanting to be somewhere else.

"Daemon taint," muttered Kluge, and Holgren nodded grimly. "I've never seen it as bad as this."

"Stupid," replied Holgren. "Mad and dangerous and stupid."

"Can we just make our way to the room the Elamner is in and get out of here?" I asked. "Then we can torch the place. From the outside." I heard a muttered agreement from some of the men behind me.

"We can try," Holgren replied, "but don't be surprised if our map is useless. This place is well on the way to becoming a hell gate. Time and space only loosely apply here now."

"Let's go," said Osskil. "Enough talk." The place was getting on even his iron nerves.

Holgren nodded assent, called up a ball of light that floated ahead of us, and set off down the corridor, Kluge and the rest of us in his wake.

The corridor was too long.

We kept walking, and walking, and by my calculations should have been off the edge of the cliff and into the Dragonsea before we came to a branching passageway on the left.

Which wasn't on the map. But was filled with blood and body parts.

There were limbs and guts and feet and fingers that had been arranged in starburst patterns on the tiled floor. There was a pile of heads. Some were still blinking. One of them was wearing my face.

"Right then," I said. "Let's go back out and try to enter the Elamner's room through the window. Dealing with Bosch can wait."

More strenuous agreement from behind me. I was becoming popular with the mercenaries.

Holgren smiled, which, considering what we were surrounded with, made me like him more, oddly. "We can try," he said. "Lord Osskil?"

Osskil was staring at a rotting arm that dragged itself toward his boot, a look of sick fascination on his heavy face. Very deliberately he raised his foot and stomped down on the black, split-nailed fingers that inched it forward. He kept stomping until the bones were shattered and the thing just lay there, quivering.

"Yes," he finally said. "Let's."

~ ~ ~

The corridor didn't lead back to the entryway anymore, we discovered after at least fifteen minutes of walking. There were no branches or turnings, but we ended up in what I suppose could be called a kitchen. Assuming hells have kitchens. There was a massive hearth, and hooks dangling from the ceiling, piercing lumps of dripping flesh, swaying in an unfelt breeze. The hearth was cold, but a vaguely human form turned on the spear-like spit, charred and blackened. It didn't have a head.

The vast floor was covered in shit and offal and bile. It was utterly silent in that space, except for the faint squeaking of the rusty chains the hooks dangled from. The ceiling was lost in gloom.

A door stood at the far side of the room. Holgren marched toward it, magelight above his head. We were forced to follow or be left in the dark, though nobody, I'm sure, was keen to kick through the awful muck that covered the floor.

We were about halfway across the room when flames exploded in the hearth, roaring and glowing a hellish green-blue.

Then things began bursting out of the floor, flinging flagstones out of their way as they rose.

They were all different as far as I could tell, but each was vaguely insectile in appearance; chitinous bodies and soulless, jet-black faceted eyes, and lots and lots of stingers and pincers and barbed, multi-jointed legs. The biggest was about the size of a lapdog. But there were a lot of them.

"Back!" shouted Holgren, reversing his course toward the corridor. One of the creatures sprang for his face and he slapped it down, earning a bloody gash on his palm.

It was chaotic. Our group fell back in fairly good order, considering, but the floor was slick with filth and the creatures just kept coming. A little one, scorpion-like, stabbed its stinger down into my boot, but didn't manage to pierce down into flesh and got itself stuck. I stomped on it awkwardly with my other foot, nearly lost my balance. One of the armsmen gave me a steadying hand. The halberdiers, competent at their trade, had moved to deal with the creatures as they came at us in waves. They looked like hells' grass cutters, their halberds mowing down the vile things, scythe-like.

"Move, now, let's go," I heard Osskil say. And then I heard rattling in the chains above.

It looked like a giant crab, more or less, but moved with the speed and grace of a spider. It was bigger than me. And it was not alone.

"Keep moving!" Holgren yelled, just before a strand of what looked like vile yellow mucus shot down from above and hit him in the chest. He made a disgusted face and cut it with a terse gesture and a harsh magical syllable. Then another came down, and another, and suddenly it was raining the stuff. Men were being hit left and right—and it was sticking, and they were being pulled upward.

Demon crabs spin mucus webs, I thought. *This is knowledge I could live my whole life without.*

The first of our group to die that day was one of the arquebusiers. A strand shot down into his face and yanked him upwards into darkness. I could hear his muffled screaming. Then I could hear the crunch of a demon taking a bite out of him, followed immediately by the thunderous roar of his weapon. They both fell to the floor, unmoving, with considerable portions of their anatomy missing.

Our group had split into two during the initial attack, I realized. Holgren, Kluge, Osskil and two swordsmen were in the group closest to the hearth, while I and the rest of the mercenaries were more than a half-dozen strides away, closer to the corridor we'd entered the room from. I didn't like not being with the mages.

But Holgren and Kluge seemed to have it in hand. Holgren was blasting everything with fire, causing charred crab-bits to rain down, and Kluge had manifested some sort of whip made of light and was slicing through the strands and keeping our people from being yanked up into the darkness above. We were all still moving toward the exit.

The closer we got to the edge of the room, the less we were affected by the disgusting onslaught from above, which was intensifying around Holgren's group. The gap between us widened, and by the time we made it to the corridor, Holgren and the others were more than a dozen strides away.

Holgren caught my eye. "Go! We'll follow!" he said.

The second of our little army to die was a halberdier.

We were all so busy watching what was going on with Holgren and the others that no one had thought to keep an eye on the corridor. So Bosch, or what Bosch had become, just walked up and speared the man in the back. I only knew we were still in danger when I heard the man scream. I whipped around, ready to throw a knife.

Bosch was both less and more than he had been before Holgren had turned his body into a large red dampness. His head was the only thing organic about him. The rest of him was some mad melding of metal and magic.

He stood perhaps seven feet tall, now. His head, smiling and eyes fever-bright, was encased in what looked like a large block of amber. It rested on a large, spider-like body made of brass and iron and steel. Small lightnings played about its frame, and actinic bursts of light coruscated across it randomly, shedding sparks.

He had run the halberdier through with one of his forelegs. The man was dangling from it, feet not quite touching the floor. He was in agony.

The mercenaries were brave, I'll give them that. They rushed towards Bosch, but he interposed the halberdier between himself and their weapons, using the dying man as a shield.

"Let him go, Bosch," I said. But he ignored me.

"How do you like my sanctum, Amra?" His voice was a series of piping notes originating from somewhere in his thorax.

"I've seen nicer slaughterhouses. Let the man go, and we might let you go."

"Is that the dead thief's fat brother I see back there? Do tell him for me how his brother screamed when I chopped his fingers off, would you? If he somehow survives. If you somehow survive."

I had nothing to say to that. I just wanted to smash the abomination that Bosch had become. I wanted to throw my knife, but doubted it could pierce the amber shell his head was encased in.

The mercenary was fading fast. He was clawing at the spike in his chest, but his movement was growing feebler by the moment.

"What to do, what to do? Will you deal with me, thief? Or will you deal with *that*?" He pointed with another blood-spattered brass leg back toward the room where Holgren and the others were trapped.

"Oh, come on. Do you think I was born last night?" As if I was going to turn my back on him. Then I heard it.

A rumbling, grinding sound.

Then a voice that was not a voice, but a presence in my head.

The Gate opens. But it is a tight fit, as yet.

I risked a quick glance back.

The demon webs were falling furiously, now. Kluge was keeping the area around their group relatively clear, his light-whip in constant, lashing motion, but it seemed almost impossible that those of us in the corridor could re-join them without becoming trapped. Still, I could see them, and the hellfire of the hearth. And the thing that was slowly tearing its way through it. Like some giant, bloated caterpillar with corpse-colored flesh. Holgren stood before it.

I felt it coming and darted to the side. Bosch's needle-sharp leg speared the air where my chest had just been.

"Worth a try," said Bosch in his calliope voice, and then he flung the now-dead halberdier at us and started loping down the corridor away from us, a horrid, drunken spider.

Holgren Angrado. You meet us half-way. This is... pleasant. Like a deep, cracked bell ringing in my head, I heard the voice of the demon

Holgren faced. I turned around again, torn.

Holgren glanced back at us.

"Go, get Bosch!" he shouted, and then he turned to face the thing that was making its way out of the hearth. He rolled his head, stretched his shoulders, like a brawler about to enter the ring. Then he spoke a harsh syllable, and there was a sound like thunder, and the demon roared in pain and rage.

Reluctantly, I went, feeling relieved I did not have to face that thing, and feeling as though I were a coward, and determined to take it out on Bosch.

"Let's go," I said to the men with me. And we went, pounding down the hall after him. He may not have been steady on his many legs, but he was swift. We didn't lose sight of him in that long, straight corridor, but we couldn't seem to gain on him, either.

Then suddenly there was a door ahead, plain blonde wood and horribly out of place. He lost time opening it, and even more time trying to fit through it. He just had time to slam it shut before we got there.

I tore the door open. Or tried to. It was locked.

"You're a thief, right?" asked one of the swordsmen, barely out of his teens. "You gonna pick the lock?"

"The hells with that. Take too long. You're hefty, give it a good kick."

"Aye." His massive booted foot lashed out and something cracked.

"Again!"

It took three more kicks, then the door sprang open with a juddering sound.

Beyond was a room I recognized, despite the gloom. The one with the corpse sporting a knife in his heart.

Bosch was crouched over the ensorcelled corpse, his own spidery brass body humming and shivering with eldritch energies. With his head mounted atop that grotesque thing, he should have looked blackly ridiculous. He didn't. He looked vile, mad, and dangerous.

"I want you to meet my employer," he said in that pipe organ voice. "You won't like him." And two delicate, shimmering spider legs plucked the dagger from the Elamner's heart.

He came up screaming, knocking Bosch into a corner. The look in his eyes was feral. Mad. Both the angry kind and the crazy kind. He saw the armed guards surrounding him, and disappeared.

Blood and chaos ensued.

I have never seen anyone move as fast as him. I suppose technically I didn't actually see him move at all. Maybe the faintest of blurrings in the air. My eyes couldn't track him.

Osskil's little army, the ones with me and not stuck in that chamber of horrors with Holgren, started to die.

There were eight armsmen in the room with me. In three heartbeats they were all falling to the floor, throats slit, bloody handprints covering their surprised faces.

And then it was my turn.

He just appeared before me, a knife in his hand. The tip of the knife pressed ever so delicately against the skin over my carotid artery.

"Abanon-touched," he said.

"Whatever you say. You're the one with the blade."

"No. *You* have Her Blade. Or you did. I can smell it on you. You must give me the Blade. Or I will kill you."

"I have no idea what you're talking about. I truly wish I did."

He sniffed again, shuddered. His lip curled. "I also smell an arhat."

"If you say so." It's not like the bald kid rubbed himself up against me.

"Do you believe I will kill you?"

"Very much so. But I still don't have Abanon's Blade."

His eyes bored into mine. "You're not lying. So you must be mistaken." Suddenly he shuddered again, violently. His face went pale. "I will find you again. When I do, you will have found the Blade. Or you will be very unhappy in the brief span before you die." And then he vanished. The window shutters rocked slightly in the breeze caused by his passage.

"Kerf's crusty old balls," I swore, and looked around the room.

Bosch had disappeared as well. All the men who had come with me were dead, and the bloody handprint on their faces was the signature of the most feared, deadly assassin in the world. Red Hand.

Heirus the Elamner was Red Hand, and he wanted me to give him something I didn't have, or he was going to kill me.

CHAPTER 23

"The Elamner is awake, and he's Red Hand the assassin," I told Holgren as he came through the door a few seconds later. I may have been gibbering, just a little.

"Yes, we managed to deal with the demon, thanks very much for ask—" He saw the bodies littering the floor. "What happened here?"

"I told you, Heirus is *Red Hand*. Bosch pulled the knife out of his chest and woke him up. He killed everybody. He wants me to give him Abanon's Blade or he's going to kill me too."

I watched him chew on it for a moment, then decide what question to ask first.

"Where's Heirus now?"

"Gone. But he said he'd find me again."

"We'll deal with it. We *will*, Amra. Where is Bosch?"

"I don't know. He disappeared when Red Hand started slaughtering everybody. Bosch is, uh, different now."

"I know, I caught a glimpse. It should limit his options for hiding at least. I don't see him renting a room, or doing much of anything where people can see him."

While I spoke to Holgren, Osskil posted one of the remaining armsmen at the window and the other at the door. Kluge was inspecting the bodies and the circle that Heirus—Red Hand—had been resting in. Professional curiosity, I suppose.

"First things first," said Osskil. "We need to do something about this house of horrors."

"Agreed," said Holgren.

"Good idea," I chimed in. "How do you close a hell mouth, by the way?"

"With fire, of course," said Kluge. "Fire with fire. But then you have to seal it, lest some other mad idiot reopens it."

"And how do you do that?" I asked him.

He shrugged. "With magic, and lots and lots of very big, very heavy rocks."

"That's for another day," said Osskil. "First let's get our dead out of this foul place, then burn it to the ground."

~ ~ ~

Kluge and one of the armsmen made sure nobody sneaked up on us while we hauled the bodies of the rest through the window. It was the shortest route, and besides, no one wanted to chance those hallways again. I agreed in principle; I didn't like to think of those dead men resting in the ashes of that house. I may not have known them, but I didn't have to, to want them out of there. But I was less enthusiastic about having to haul the bodies.

I'm not particularly squeamish. It wasn't handling their corpses that bothered me. It was seeing that bloody handprint on those dead faces, and knowing it might very well be me next. If Red Hand wanted me dead, then I was dead. If even a fraction of the tales told about him were true, he'd been around for generations, dealing death to kings and queens, priests and generals, merchants and even godlings all around the Dragonsea. He would disappear for years, then the all-but-impossible assassinations would start again, all with that signature bloody handprint. Red Hand was literally the stuff that legends—and nightmares—were made of.

When we'd shifted all the corpses that Red Hand had made, I turned to Osskil.

"I hate to say it, but there are two more in there." The arquebusier the demon crab had killed, and the halberdier Bosch had done for.

"I know," he said, "but we dare not risk more deaths to recover them." He shook his head. "We were not prepared. I was not prepared, not for this. We should not have continued once we knew what this place had turned into."

"I don't think it would have mattered if we'd brought a hundred men," I told him, "or a dozen mages. You didn't see how Red Hand moved. Eight men dead in the space of three heartbeats. There is no preparing for a foe like that."

He just shook his head.

"We should have burned the place to the ground right off," he said. "Never even entered at all."

"But then you'd never have known for certain Corbin's killer was done for. He might've been out having a shave when you came calling."

"I could live with that. In retrospect. I went looking to avenge one death. Now there are ten more, and my brother's murderer no closer to being dealt with."

"Such talk does not become you, Lord Osskil."

He raised an eyebrow. "That sounded rather haughty."

I shrugged and pointed towards Holgren. "Been spending too much time around that one."

It got a smile out of him at least.

~ ~ ~

Holgren and Kluge reduced the villa with magefire, which for the most part looked like normal fire. Except, you know, it was being blasted out of their hands. It *was* especially bright, even in the dim predawn light. I noted with some satisfaction that Kluge had to quit halfway through. He looked as though he'd run from the Dragon Gate to the Governor's Palace without stopping. Admittedly, Holgren didn't look much better when he'd finished. I'd have made a joke, but neither mage looked like they were in the mood.

The stench from the burning villa was more than awful, and the breeze coming off the Dragonsea was light but variable; more than once it shifted direction unexpectedly, and the vile smoke reduced Holgren or Kluge to gasping retches. It was not a pleasant chore, and to the credit of both they never complained once.

While they were about it, the rest of us loaded the dead into the omnibus along with the prisoners. Alain wasn't going to be happy about the blood. Alain would get over it.

I took a water skin from one of the men and gave it to Holgren, who was surveying the ruins of the villa. He took it with a grateful look and drank deep.

"So. You think Bosch is in there?" I asked him.

"I'm afraid not." He pulled out the compass he'd prepared with Bosch's hair. The needle pointed due East.

"I don't understand. It's pointing at the house. Or what's left of it."

"If only it were. If he were as close as that, the needle would be spinning aimlessly. He's much farther away."

"But that's the Dragonsea."

"Precisely. He doesn't need to breathe, and there isn't much to him anymore to attract a hungry pheckla."

"Kerf's balls. He's well and truly beyond reach then, isn't he?"

"Yes. For now. That one won't be content to scuttle along the sea bed for long, however. We will see him again, and sooner rather than later."

~ ~ ~

I was deeply, deeply tired. I parted company with the others as soon as we got into the Spindles, and headed toward another one of my bolt-holes to sleep, after promising to check in with Osskil and Holgren the next day. I don't know what Kluge and Osskil did with the Elamner's guards, or with the bodies. I also don't know what Myra and Alain thought about the condition they received their omnibus in. It was all in one piece, though, so they couldn't have been too upset.

I probably should have gone with Holgren to his sanctum, but it was just too far. Instead I trudged over to the herbalist's whose back room I rented and sneaked in the window.

As I crawled under the single dusty sheet that graced the cot in the dark, funny-smelling back room of the herbalist's, though, one thought kept nagging at me.

It was a little thing, and it probably meant nothing, but it kept me awake for a considerable time considering how exhausted and sleep-deprived I was. You'd think it was Red Hand, and his demand that I give him something I had no idea how to get, but it was something else.

Bosch. Gloating about chopping off Corbin's fingers.

Sure, it was a nasty thing, calculated to enrage, horrible enough in its own way. But why gloat about that and not the actual murder? Why not talk about letting him run, as Kluge had mentioned, and hunting him down like an animal? That was just as cruel, if not more so.

It was a small thing, but it didn't fit.

Something was missing. Something was off.

CHAPTER 24

I slept until noon, then left the herbalist's the way I came. What the old woman thought about her mysterious boarder I couldn't say. The room was paid up months in advance and the door triple-locked from the inside, which must have seemed odd, but not odd enough to turn down easy money. That's one thing I like about Lucernans; once money changes hands, they become deeply uncurious.

At Osskil's manse I was informed that I was invited to another funeral. Or funerals, rather. Three of the armsmen he'd hired had no one to claim their bodies, and so he'd decided to inter them in the Thracen crypt reserved for retainers. It was, apparently, a rather gracious gesture on his part. They'd have a posher afterlife than they would've had otherwise, at least. It was scheduled for the late afternoon. I wasn't all that keen on going, but Osskil wouldn't be available until then. I was led to believe by his servant that he was off getting scolded by Lord Morno again.

I decided to have a very late, or rather for me a very early breakfast. At which point I realized I was thoroughly broke. I didn't trust Holgren to have any food, and didn't want to walk all the way to his house in any case, so I decided to kill two birds with one stone and get a meal and an advance from Daruvner. I'd promised to check in with him anyway.

It was quiet at his dive. No nieces, no Kettle, and very few patrons. Daruvner fed me, loaned me a few marks and then insisted I tell him everything that had been going on.

"You don't want to know," I said.

"I think I do."

I shrugged. "On your head, then, old man," I said, then filled him in about Corbin, how I'd decided to go after his killer, and how things had gone straight to hells. He supplied me with wine as I wound through the whole sordid mess, and when I was done he sat back, stared up at the water-stained, sagging plaster on the ceiling and idly rubbed his massive belly.

"There's something I don't understand," he finally said.

"You're ahead of me, then. I'm starting to feel like I don't understand anything."

"'Thus wisdom grows; in stony, unaccustomed soil,'" he replied.

"I don't know what you're talking about, but I'm sure it wasn't flattering."

"Just a quote. Look, you don't even know who killed Corbin."

"The hells I don't."

"Hear me out, woman. You've pinned this on Bosch, and his boss Heirus—"

"Call him what he really is. Red Hand."

"I'm not sure I believe that, but say that he is. Bosch admitted to cutting off Corbin's fingers, but never said anything about killing him, correct?"

"Yeah," I admitted. "That's been bothering me. But his boss is Red Hand, Daruvner. You know, king of assassins? Maybe Bosch didn't do it. Doesn't mean his boss didn't."

"You say you saw this Elamner kill a half-dozen men right in front of you. You say you know it was Red Hand because he put his bloody mark on their faces. Correct?"

"It was eight men, actually, but yes."

Daruvner leaned forward, locked eyes with me. "Did Corbin have Red Hand's mark?"

I wanted it to be the Elamner. After all the blood and trouble, I wanted it to be the obvious bad guy. But the truth is the truth, and facts are facts.

"No. Damn it."

He leaned back again, chair creaking under his weight. "I'm not saying he didn't do it. I'm not saying Bosch didn't do it. I'm not even saying it wasn't hired out by one or the other of them. What I am saying is, you've been mistaking what you think for what you know. You wouldn't do that on a job. You've let your anger cloud your judgment like you never would if this was business."

"It's not business, Fengal. Somebody killed my friend. How can I treat it as though it was just another theft?"

'But it *is* just another theft," he replied, his voice mild. "You're going to take something. Something valuable. You're going to take someone's life. You're going to take revenge. Here's where I'm very much starting to worry for you though, Amra: The consequences of a mistake on your part are the same as if you were caught lifting a cask of jewels: Death. And in this case, I'm sorry to say, you're not even sure you've got the right mark."

"A daemonist who was just about to open a hell gate on the Jacos Road and his boss, the king of assassins. I may have got the wrong villains. *May* have. But they're still villains, Fengal."

"Since when is it your job to deal with evil, Amra? You're a thief, not a hells-damned knight of the Order of the Oak. And consider this, please; while you're keeping the world safe from these very bad men, it's more than possible that your friend's real killer is out there, safe, satisfied."

"Well it's a little late now. Bosch came after me first, and I doubt Red Hand is going to leave me alone just because I say sorry and pretty please."

He rubbed his shiny head and sighed. "What can I say? You should have come and talked to me sooner. I'm deeply wise of course, but sadly I cannot undo what's already done. You've already pulled on trouble's braids."

"If you're so wise, old man, why don't you tell me who you think it was that killed Corbin?"

"True wisdom lies not in knowing the correct answer, but in knowing the correct question."

"Fine. Be that way. I've got to go. I've got three funerals to attend." I stood up.

"Don't you want to know the correct question?" he asked.

I sighed. No, I didn't. All right, yes I did, but I didn't have to be happy about it. "Sure, why not."

"Who had reason to want Corbin killed, besides the two new enemies you've made?"

"That's just it, Fengal. I have no idea."

"Well then maybe you should start trying to find out. When you have time."

"Yeah, when I have time."

"And for Isin's love, get over to Locquewood's and pick up your package. He's been bothering me about it for days, now."

"When I have time, old man!" I said as I went through the door.

CHAPTER 25

I t wasn't quite as nice as Corbin's crypt, but the mausoleum for the Thracen retainers was still much more classy than any final resting place I was likely to end up in.

I met Osskil, the same three professional mourners, and two of the surviving armsmen in the necropolis in the late afternoon, about an hour before sunset. Holgren had sent his regrets and funerary tokens, claiming 'unavoidable occupation.' I think he just didn't like funerals, for all that he lived next to dead bodies.

The funeral table was bigger, but the whole ceremony was pretty much the same as for Corbin. Someone had washed the Red Hand's mark off their faces, thank the gods, and sewed them up with care. They were wearing good cloth under good armor, and their weapons were with them, shiny and sharp.

I arrived in time for the meal, which was all right. Simple fare, no meat. The three professional mourners, I found out, were brothers, though they each had different surnames; Wallum, Stumpole and Brock. I didn't try to puzzle that one out. I had enough on my mind.

Osskil made the ceremonial speech, we drank the funerary wine, and suddenly there they were, for a few moments, no longer corpses. The youngest one, the one that had kicked in the door to his own doom, looked at me with a sheepish grin on his face. Another, the one in the middle, just looked befuddled. The one on the end, a swordsman, was obviously angry, though somehow I knew it was not at us.

We toasted them, and they raised their glasses at us, the one in the middle having to be nudged by the younger one. And then they were just bodies again, and we put them in the mausoleum in the golden afternoon light.

Once the doors were closed, I turned to Osskil.

"On the day Corbin was killed, Kluge and the constables went through his house."

He nodded. "I know. I was told."

"Then you know what they found?" The letter, which according to Kluge, meant that Corbin might have been invited back into the family. That, and a Thracen signet ring. Daruvner's words had been bothering me the whole trip to the Necropolis. Who had reason to want Corbin killed?

"I know they found evidence he was a thief, and the letter I'd sent him, along with his family ring. Why?"

"The letter *you* sent him?"

"Certainly. Again, why?"

"What did the letter say?"

"I'm not sure that's your business, Amra. It's a family matter, and as much as I like you, you aren't family."

"But I was his friend, and so I'm asking you to tell me what was in the letter."

He gave me a long, hard look. "This cannot be shared with anyone else."

"You've got my word."

"My father is head of the family, but he is no longer in control of his faculties in any meaningful way. I control our interests, now, and make the family decisions. And now that my father is in no condition to object, I want— wanted my brother back. I wanted him to return to the family, to his home, to his daughter if not his wife. I wanted him to be able to be a part of her childhood, while there was still something of her childhood left. It was just too late."

I felt ashamed for doubting him. It wasn't as if Corbin, being the younger brother, could have inherited while Osskil was alive anyway.

"Now will you tell me why you wanted to know?" he asked, sounding more weary and heartsick than angry.

I really didn't want to answer him. For several reasons. But I owed him.

"There's a chance Bosch and Heirus didn't kill Corbin," I said.

"But what does that—" His eyes grew hard. "You suspected *me*?"

"No. Not really. But I wanted to make sure. You would have done the same."

That hard, cold look of his softened. "I suppose I would have, at that. But why do you think the killer might be someone else?"

"I'll tell you about it later," I said, my mouth suddenly dry and my palms sweaty.

About twenty yards away, Heirus had suddenly appeared and was staring straight at me.

Osskil hadn't noticed him there. I wanted to keep it that way. I turned away, walking slowly towards the crypt, and Osskil kept pace.

"Can I come by tomorrow?" I asked. "I'll lay it all out for you then."

"Certainly. I'll be in all day. But why not now?"

"Because I need to do some thinking first."

He gave me a long, penetrating stare. I tried to show him nothing. Finally he nodded, and started walking towards the exit. Everybody else had been waiting for him, and followed.

As the mourners streamed off towards the gate, I picked my way around headstones and past mausoleums towards Heirus. Night wasn't far off. The sun was already behind the high walls, casting everything into half-gloom

He was standing at the base of the very large, not very lovely statue of the Weeping Mother. His oiled, ringleted hair glistened dully in the half-light. His gaunt, dusky face betrayed no emotion.

"I don't have the Blade," I said to him. "I don't know where it is. I'm not holding out on you."

He seemed not to hear me. He was staring right at me, but he made no acknowledgement. I kept moving toward him, slow and careful, the way you approach any wild, dangerous animal. If you have no choice.

"Have you ever hated? *Really* hated, with every fiber of your being?" he finally asked me as I came within spitting distance of him. "True hate is a powerful thing. It can give you the strength of will to do things you never would have considered. Things you never would have believed yourself capable of. Unthinkable things. Awful and magnificent things." He took a deep breath, let it out slow. "Hate is a powerful force because it lends an impossible strength. With enough hate, you could rule the world. Or end it."

"Is that what you want to do?" I asked him. "Destroy the world?"

He laughed. "I don't give a runny shit about the world, or anyone or anything in it."

"Then by all the dead gods, what *do* you want?"

He sat down, heavily, on a cracked headstone across from me; leaned down and put his forearms on his knees. He looked tired and ill.

"I think," I said, "that you're sick. Maybe dying. I think you want the Blade because it will somehow cure you."

He laughed.

"What's so funny?"

"You think I'm dying. You don't know the half of it. *I die a dozen times a day.*"

"That sounds unpleasant."

"Well, curses aren't meant to be enjoyable. It's what I got for slaying a god."

"Um, out of curiosity, which god did you kill?'

He gave me an annoyed look. "One who needed it. One whose siblings took offense." He shuddered, looked as though he might vomit. It passed.

"How long have you been cursed?" I asked.

"How old do you think I am?" he asked.

"Forty? Maybe forty-five?"

"I'm seventeen hundred years old. Older than the Cataclysm. I saw the fall of Thagoth, and of Hluria. I was ancient when Havak Silversword was imprisoned behind the Wall. You people are mayflies to me."

"You're tired of life."

"You haven't the least idea. It's much worse than it sounds. Because of the curse laid on me, every moment that passes feels like a hundred. Listening to you talk bores me to tears. Listening to *me* talk bores me to tears. I've experienced this conversation as though it's lasted all damned day."

"I'll try and talk faster," I said, but he waved it away.

"Don't bother. You can't speak quickly enough to make the slightest difference."

"So what do you want, Heirus?"

Suddenly he was in my face. I never saw him move.

"I want the Goddess's gods-damned Blade, you stupid cow!"

"Call me a cow again and I'll stick the Blade so far up your—"

I never saw the fist, either.

I sprawled on the ground and in that bright flare of pain realization came to me.

"The toad," I said. "It's in the toad." Though if there was a weapon inside the thing, it wasn't a very big one. Maybe suitable for paring nails. But when it came to magical artifacts, who knew what was possible?

I wanted to spit out the blood that was spilling into my mouth from the torn lining of my cheek, but I remembered what Osskil had told me. You don't shed blood in the Necropolis. Ever. The Guardian *will* notice. I swallowed it instead.

"Yes, it's in the toad. Nice to see you're finally catching up."

"Kerf's crooked staff. You're worse than that priest of Lagna."

"I don't know or care what you're talking about. Just get me the toad and we can be shut of each other."

"The thing you had Corbin murdered for? I'd sooner see it dumped in the Dragonsea than in your hands."

"Your mouth moves but no sense escapes."

"You had Corbin killed so you wouldn't have to pay his fee for securing the toad. Then you put a contract out on me so you could have a necromancer get the toad's location out of my corpse. Am I making sense now?" I wasn't certain of anything I was saying, of course, but he didn't have to know that.

"Oh. I see. You're laboring under a misapprehension. I didn't have your friend killed, or hire killers to end you either. Perhaps Bosch got greedy and decided to keep the fee for himself. I don't know. I don't care."

"Why should I belie—" I didn't get to finish my sentence. A knife had appeared at my throat, pressing hard enough to draw a drop of blood. Then it was at my heart. Then almost, almost touching my eye. It didn't waver in the slightest in his hand.

"If I'd wanted your friend dead, or you dead, I wouldn't have bothered paying for it. Understand?"

"Yes."

"Finally." He stood up from where he was crouched over me. "If for some idiotic reason I'd wanted to kill your compatriot, who I hired to *retrieve* the damned toad, I'd have done it *after* I'd secured the Blade. If somehow I'd become doltish enough to make a botch of *that*, I'd have brought the cooling meat of him to a necromancer straight away. And while

Bosch may not be the brightest spark in the firmament, he's cunning enough to work out the same. Now. Bring me the Blade here at dawn tomorrow. Or I *will* find and kill you, and drag your corpse to a necromancer and make you tell me where you've hidden it. I will also kill both the mages and that fat lord that invaded my home."

"Alright. One condition, though." What did I have to lose?

He gave me a flat, put-upon stare.

"Go to Guache Gavon and tell him to cancel the contract on me."

"Who?"

"The Low Country trash that arranges contracts for assassination here. Or are you going to tell me that Red Hand doesn't know what I'm talking about?"

"Oh. I know him. His name escaped me."

"Tell him the contract lapsed with Bosch. Or tell him you cancel it. Whatever. I just don't want to be dodging assassins while I get the toad and bring it to you."

"Fair," he said. "I *will* see you tomorrow. One day," he said again.

"Where do we meet?"

"Just come here. I'll find you. So don't bother to run. And keep that Arhat away from me or I'll eviscerate him."

"The bald kid?" I didn't have to feign confusion. I knew who he meant, but had no idea why he wanted to avoid a teenaged ascetic. It was a strange tic of character for the King of Assassins to have. "It's not like I have him on a leash," I said, but I said it to the air. Heirus was gone.

CHAPTER 26

"**D**o you want to give it to him?" Holgren asked me when I returned to his sanctum and related my conversation.

"Do I have a choice? He's *Red Hand*, for Kerf's sweet sake. I don't give it to him, I'm a dead woman."

"That isn't what I asked, though. Do you *want* to give it to him?" The toad was sitting in the middle of some sort of arcane circle he'd sketched out on the floor with charcoal and blood. Bone wanted nothing to do with it, and kept to the corner farthest away.

"I want to have never seen that ugly thing. Sometimes we don't get what we want."

"If there is a weapon inside it, a blade forged by a goddess..."

"What?"

"When you next meet the most feared assassin in history, wouldn't you like to be holding it, rather than an ugly lump of gold?"

I sighed. "Hells, I don't know, Holgren. He'd probably just take it away from me and shove it in my ear. You didn't see the way he moves. Neither did I, for that matter, if I'm speaking precisely."

"Logically speaking, your choice is between meeting him essentially unarmed, or holding a powerful weapon. I know which I'd chose, but it's up to you. As for his speed, I think I can help you there as well. At least for a short time."

"Magic?"

"Of course." He dipped two fingers into the pocket of his waistcoat and brought out a pendant on a silver chain. The pendant was in the shape of a leaf, made of silver as well, about the size of my thumb.

"You just happened to have it in your pocket, eh?"

He smiled. "After what happened at the villa, I decided to un-crate some of my more useful, if dangerous, items."

"Speaking of the villa, that thing that crawled out of the hearth? It knew your name."

His face went hard. "Yes, it did."

"Did you want to talk about that, maybe?"

"Not particularly, no. Suffice it to say that, while I have had dealings with such creatures, I am no daemonist. If that is what you wanted to know."

I raised a hand. "Not my business."

"No, I understand that you might be concerned. Be at ease on that score." He sighed. "Back to the matter at hand," he went on, holding up the necklace.

"What is it?"

"I've made a study of longevity. Call it an interest of mine. In my studies I came across a way to, shall we say, live more expeditiously for a short time. At the cost of shortening your own lifespan commensurately.

"Can you say that without all the expensive words?"

He smiled. "It lets you cram an entire day or so of living into roughly an hour. At the end of the hour, you're a day older."

"Oh. That's not bad. I could even see giving up a week, or even a month."

"It would kill you. The aftereffects are brutal. Imagine not sleeping, eating or drinking for an entire day and night. Bad enough. A week? You might well die of thirst. A month? You'd be dead before the spell wore off. But if you need to, you can. The spell *will* let you. Best if you don't need to."

"Magic comes with a price, eh?"

"Always. Though some don't count the cost until it is too late." His expression became remote, but he quickly shrugged off whatever he was thinking about and put the chain around my neck. "No need to decide this instant. If you want to use it, just break the chain."

I thought about it while scratching Bone behind the ear. With the weapon inside the toad and Holgren's magic, I might stand a chance against Heirus. Without either I stood none, and would have to trust him not to kill me out of hand. And I still had no idea what he wanted to do with it. I honestly could not imagine it would be anything remotely good.

I was starting to believe—reluctantly—that he had not had Corbin killed. All right, he almost certainly hadn't. If I was honest with myself, I didn't want to let go of the notion of him as the culprit because he so obviously fit the mould. And because if he hadn't been the cause of Corbin's death, then there was someone else out there who was. Someone I was no closer to finding than I had been at the beginning.

That did not make him a nice person. The Red Hand had killed more people than famine had, if you believed only half the stories about him. Hells.

"Alright," I said. "Let's open up that ugly thing and get Abanon's Blade out."

"That would be a very bad idea," said the bald boy as he walked through Holgren's door, and wards, as though they didn't exist.

~ ~ ~

"Who are you and how did you gain entry to my sanctum?" Holgren's voice was calm, but I could tell he was ready and willing to unleash violence.

I recognized the boy, of course. The ascetic who had been staring at me as I left Alain's place. The one from the funeral. Arhat.

"Gaining entry to your sanctum was not difficult, magus. Magic is a rusty hammer with which to beat reality into different shapes. Philosophy, the true Philosophy, is a pen with which to alter, and hopefully correct reality."

"Arhat," said Holgren. The boy nodded.

"What do you want?"

"Please give me the statue. It is not meant for you. It is not meant for the world."

"You know this kid?" I asked Holgren.

"I've never laid eyes on him."

"But you know his name."

"Arhat? That's not a name. It's a title." He had a pissy expression on his lean face.

"Alright, I'll bite. What's an Arhat?"

"Do you remember the Cataclysm?" he asked.

"Not really, no. It *was* a thousand years ago." But he wasn't in any mood for banter.

"If you want to know why the Cataclysm happened, ask the Arhat."

I looked over at the kid. He shook his head sadly. "The Cataclysm was not the fault of the Philosophers, mage."

"Oh really? Then who was it that decided to poke and prod at the underpinnings of reality? Milk maids?"

"No. But not the Philosophers, either. A group that perverted Philosophy—"

"The point remains, Arhat, if those wise fools hadn't gone mucking about with knowledge man was literally not meant to know, *millions* wouldn't have perished—"

"Enough," I said, rather loudly. "If you two want to debate, go to the Speaker's Corner. Kerf's crooked staff, we're under a deadline here, or had you forgotten, Holgren? Arhat, you can't have the toad. Sorry about that, now please run along."

Holgren just stood there, looking mulish. The kid refused to run along.

"Seriously, go. We don't have time for you."

"Please give me the statue. What is inside should stay there, in my safekeeping. I've been entrusted with it since I was ten years old. When it was stolen, I failed in my duty. I must take that duty up again."

"Look," I said, losing patience, "We don't have time for this. If Heirus doesn't get the Blade, lots of people are going to die, including and especially us. 'Please' is nice, but not nearly enough."

"The Blade was never meant to leave me. I am its guardian. I must have it back, or the consequences could be unimaginable."

I looked at him. "Corbin took it from you?"

"It was stolen from the temple."

"Some tumbledown place in the Gol-Shen swamps?"

"Yes."

I remembered the cryptic remark he'd made in the City of the Dead. "Then you're a shitty guardian. I wouldn't give it back to you in any case. Now get out."

"You have no idea what you're doing. Do not render down the statue, for the love of all."

"Tell me why. Give me one good reason, good enough to balance being slaughtered by the bloody Red Hand if I don't."

"It could end the very world."

"Well that's pretty good, I admit, but I have only your word on it, and besides, if we don't melt the damned thing down, Heirus will just kill us, take it, and melt it down himself. Nice try though. Holgren, let's do it. Or are you going to try and stop us, Arhat?"

"I will not attempt to force you to stop. But know this: What is inside the statue is like a psychic poison. If you release it, what little shielding there is between it and the world will be gone. Everyone and everything around it will be twisted beyond all recognition. Quick or slow, it *will* happen."

"Again, only your word."

"For seven years I have watched over Abanon's Blade. I have paid the price. I will show you."

And he did.

Suddenly he wasn't a fresh-faced boy anymore. Suddenly he was a nightmare, scaled and diseased, elongated slavering jaw, piss-colored eyes, taloned fingers—

And that now-familiar hate washed over me and I wanted him dead, dead, in pieces on the floor to stomp on until he was just a stain. I had a knife out and winging toward him in an eye blink, and was already following it with another in hand to gut him, but he was gone.

"You see?" he said from behind me, just a boy again. I spun around and saw that Holgren had a spitting, coruscating knife made of light under the boy's chin, and a slowly disappearing snarl on his face. Bone, silent as death, had sunk his ivory fangs into the boy's calf, and blood trickled down.

"The Blade that Whispers Hate," murmured the boy as Holgren, pale-faced, turned him loose and led Bone outside, shaking and querulous. "Do you think you can ignore its blandishments? I could not. If you release it, you'll find you have only two choices. To act on them, much to the world's woe, or to... internalize them." He bent down and ran a hand over his bleeding leg. The puncture wounds from Bone's fangs turned to puckered scars in front of my eyes, and the blood dried and flaked away onto Holgren's threadbare carpet. "I chose to take in the hate that leaked out of the Blade's prison, lest it poison the very air of the temple and the waters of the swamp. It forced upon me this duality, this alternate self that draws the hatred of others like a lodestone."

"Surely there was some other alternative," I said.

"None that I could think of. Do you mind if I sit?" he asked.

"Not my house, but feel free." I was trembling from the aftereffects of that blind hate. I sat, too. Holgren came back in and leaned against the door sill, regarding the Arhat with sharp, brooding eyes.

"You've attacked me twice," I said to the Arhat. "First you tried to break into my house, then you ambushed me when I was breaking into Heirus's villa. Why?"

"The first time I only meant to take the toad while you slept. But you woke. I did not attack you."

"You sure as hells did the second time."

"To keep you from entering the villa. If you had, you would have died. And my intent was not to harm you. But my control over the form Abanon cursed me with is imperfect."

"Why use it at all then?"

"It is strong. And it is impervious to pain."

"Why not just appear in my rooms and take the toad?"

He smiled. "I could not, otherwise I would have. The physical places where such parlor tricks are possible are limited, and random. To understand more I would need to teach you at least the fundamentals of Philosophy—"

"Mmm, no thanks. I'm a little pressed for time." And interest.

Holgren cleared his throat. "I agree that releasing the Blade would be imprudent," he said. "It still must be handed over to Heirus. There's no way around it."

"I implore you not to do so."

"Sorry. As Amra said, we have no choice."

"Well then, I will have to take it from him, then."

"Oh," I said. "He told me if he sees you he's going to do unpleasant things to your body."

"Be that as it may."

"You want to tell me why he hates you?"

"He hates all Arhat."

"Again, why?"

"He founded the Order of Philosophers. After the Cataclysm, he walked away from the Order, vowing eternal enmity."

"Sounds like there's a story in there."

"Oh yes. But one you do not have time to hear."

He stood up, and walked out the door. Holgren and I exchanged glances. He gave me a small shrug.

Somebody else knocked at Holgren's door.

"I'm becoming entirely too popular," he said with a frown. He put his hand to the door, shrugged, and opened it.

Standing at the door was Kettle, Daruvner's runner. Usually he had a mischievous look plastered on his round face, but tonight he was serious.

"Miss Amra, Daruvner wants to see you. Says it's urgent. You're s'posed to take the hack back with me." He pointed a pudgy thumb over his shoulder to the waiting carriage. "Magister Holgren should come too, an' it please him."

"What's it about, Kettle?"

He shook his head. "Not sure. Something to do with Locquewood. His man Bollund showed up at Fengal's door, bleeding like a fountain, asking after you."

CHAPTER 27

There wasn't much chit-chat in the hack on the way to Daruvner's. Holgren had taken the toad, no longer trusting the security of his sanctum, but left Bone.

I prodded Kettle to tell me what he knew.

"Bollund staggered in the eatery at supper time, blood gushing out'n him. Looked like he'd been speared in the guts. Looked like he was holding 'em in with his hands, truth be told." Kettle shuddered. "We got 'im into the back room, an' he was goin' on about a giant metal spider and askin' after you. Fengal sent me off to fetch a physicker from down the lane, and when I'd got back with 'im, Bollund was passed out and Fengal told me to go an' fetch you two."

"Bosch is back," I said to Holgren, and he nodded.

"Who's Bosch?" asked Kettle.

"A giant metal spider," I replied, and his eyes got big.

"I thought he was just delirious."

"Sadly, no," said Holgren.

Kettle didn't seem to want to talk much after that, and I didn't want to talk too much about what might be going on in front of him, so the rest of the ride was silent. When we got to Fengal's, Kettle paid the hack off and unlocked the door to the eatery. If I'd doubted it was serious before, I didn't now. Fengal never closed, except for private parties, which he almost never hosted.

Kettle led the way back past empty tables to a storeroom off the kitchen.

Bollund lay on a makeshift cot, covered with an old horse blanket. He wasn't conscious. He was very pale, lips ashen. Daruvner was sitting in a chair near him. When he saw us, he got up and ushered us back out into the dining room.

"So Bosch attacked Bollund?" I asked him.

"No doubt. Speared him through the back and out the belly."

"What the hells for?"

He shrugged. "Because he's a nasty little git?"

"No, why did he attack *Bollund*?"

"He knew Locquewood was Corbin's fixer, and assumed Locquewood, and by extension Bollund, would know how to contact you."

"Me?"

"Of course. He wants the toad. Bollund said he's got Locquewood hostage in his shop. He sent Bollund out to tell you to bring him the toad. Alone. If you don't, he swears he'll start killing everyone you know, starting with Locquewood."

"But I don't even like Locquewood."

"That's not funny, Amra," chided Fengal.

"I just meant it's not like he's got my lover or a family member held hostage."

"Do you happen to have a lover, or any family to take?" Holgren said.

"Well no, but—"

"Locquewood was the easiest to get to, of all the people Bosch can connect to you. I was more than his match before he entered his present state, Baron Thracen is amply protected, and Inspector Kluge is quite adept at staying alive. In any case, he knew exactly where to find Locquewood, having dealt with him for the original commission. Locquewood was low-hanging fruit."

"You need to go rescue him, Amra," said Daruvner.

"Weren't you the one who told me not to be a hero?"

"I didn't tell you to be heartless, either. Bosch is your mess to clean up now."

"I'm not saying I don't want to deal with Bosch. I have scores to settle with him. I'm just saying I'm not doing it for Locquewood. Kerf's balls."

"Well, now that we're clear on that," said Holgren, "let's be on our way, shall we? Like him or not, the longer Locquewood is subjected to the attentions of Bosch, the less likely he is to survive them."

"You're coming with me?"

"Of course. I too have unfinished business with Bosch."

~ ~ ~

Kettle whistled up a hack for us. I was amazed he found one as quickly as he did, that late at night. The ride to the Dragon gate was a short one, but by the time we got there Holgren had already sketched out a plan.

"Don't enter the shop," he said as he passed me the toad. "Just call out to him, and show him the statue if you must. As soon as I can see him, I promise you he won't be in any condition to cause further trouble."

"Well that sounds simple enough," I replied. But I privately doubted it would be so easy. Bosch was mad, but he was cunning. I couldn't see him presenting such an easy target for Holgren to destroy. I would have said so, but Holgren had displayed some seriously disturbing abilities in the way of making things dead. So I kept my mouth shut, and hoped he was right.

We alighted at the end of the deserted, lamp-lit street. Locquewood's shop was in the middle of a commercial area, high-end, and nobody bought expensive trinkets like his in the middle of the night. Holgren put a hand on my shoulder, then crossed the street. We walked the rest of the way up the slight incline to Locquewood's shop.

There were no lights on in the expensive glass display windows. The door was closed. I glanced back across the street. Holgren was nowhere to be seen, but I didn't worry that he'd taken off. Much.

I put a hand on the knob and tried it. Unlocked. I pushed it open.

"Hey, Bosch," I called. "I hear you wanted to talk to me."

Silence, then a low groan, somewhere far back in the shop.

"Anybody home?" I called.

"Come in, Amra." That pipe organ voice. "I hope you've brought me my trinket."

"I think I'll stay right here, thanks. Why don't you come and get what you wanted?" I held up the toad.

"Bring it to me," said Bosch. "Now."

"No."

Locquewood screamed. Quite a lot.

"My new limbs lack digits, but they are the very thing for poking out eyes, I've found."

"What the hells is wrong with you, Bosch?"

"Having my body disintegrated has made me churlish. Now bring me the toad, or this dandy will lose his other eye. And I should warn you, my limbs are not really suited for fine work. It's entirely possible I'll poke too deep."

"Kerf's crooked staff," I swore. I shoved the toad inside my jacket and pulled out my knives. And entered the spider's web.

CHAPTER 28

"You might as well let the dandy go," I said as I stepped into the dark interior of the shop. "It's you and I that have this dance."

I walked slowly past rows of precious gewgaws and delicate frippery, giving my eyes time to adjust to the gloom. The shop wasn't all that big; I was certain Bosch and Locquewood were in the back room. The muted witchlight that pulsed erratically from the dark interior was another clue.

"All right," he said. "Mister Locquewood, if you would care to depart, be my guest."

A dull whimper was the only reply.

"It seems Mister Locquewood prefers sitting in a puddle of his own blood, Amra."

"Come out here, Bosch, and get your toad." Here at least there was some light from the street. The storeroom was windowless.

"Come back and hand it to me."

"Let's stop the games. You plan on killing me and Locquewood both, and taking the idol. I'm willing to try and save him, but not at the cost of my own life. I'm more than willing to meet you half-way, though, if you come out here now and face me. Then whoever's left standing does whatever they want."

"So you aren't going to come back here to save this wretch's life?"

I didn't like where that question was headed. "Are you afraid to face me?"

There was a jarring series of notes that I decided was Bosch's new laugh.

"I'll take that as a no. Come out. We'll settle our difference. Since you're certain of the outcome, you can always go back and finish Locquewood off after you've sorted me out."

"That would just be extra work," he replied, and then I heard a wet tearing sound, and an agonized scream that abruptly cut off.

"Oh, dear," said Bosch. "Clumsy me."

One of the things I was taught, long ago in the back alleys of Bellarius when Theiner, my friend and protector was teaching me to fight with knives, was to never, ever lose your temper in a fight. Of all the knife fighting techniques he drilled me on, that one was the most crucial. It was a hard lesson for me to learn—for any child to learn—but learn it I did.

I surprised myself a little with the hot splash of rage that sprang up at Locquewood's death. I hadn't liked him but he certainly hadn't deserved to be tortured to death. I'd like to think anyone would have felt the same, but sadly I knew better. That detached, emotionless part of my mind began to churn out bare facts in rapid succession despite my emotion.

Locquewood was almost certainly dead or on the way. My reason for being in this trap had expired. Time to leave. Holgren could burn the place down once I was out of it.

I turned and ran. Not a moment too soon, as it turned out.

Bosch had kept control of one of his hellish pets. It had been above me the entire time I was talking, waiting to drop down on me.

As I turned, I caught the barest flicker of movement from above, and then its talons raked my back, ripping my jacket and the shirt and skin beneath to ribbons. The daemonette that had retrieved Bosch's head from Gavon's. The shock of it forced a cry of pain out of me, but I kept moving. Holgren, and light enough to see my enemy, were just outside the door.

I heard a hiss and a scrabbling of talons on the hardwood floor. I knew the thing was disgustingly fast. Probably fast enough to get hold of me before I made it outside. No time to turn and cast a knife. So I turned my lunge into a sort of pirouette as I reached the door, knife arm extending out to where I imagined it would be.

I got it in the throat.

It ripped my forearm all to hells, and when we landed in the street, it was on top of me. My knife in its neck kept it from biting my face off, though it still strained fiercely to get its slavering, beetly jaws on me. Its claws were starting to do to my front what they'd done to my back, though, scoring lines of blood and fire down my chest and belly.

I got another knife into its side with my left hand. Using the two knife hilts as handles, I rolled over and arched my body away from its talons. However fierce it was, I had the weight advantage. I got it mostly on its back. Carefully, I put a boot to its neck and put my weight down on it as it twisted and writhed.

Then I pulled out both my blades and with speed and precision borne of long, long practice, I planted one in each of its faceted eyes, until the tips grated against the back of its skull.

"That's for Locquewood, I suppose," I panted, then sprang back, knives in hand. It thrashed a moment more, and was suddenly still.

Bosch faced me from the doorway.

"Impressive," he piped. "I would clap, but, you know." He raised his two blood-stained forelimbs, waggled them back and forth. Then he attacked. *Where the hells is Holgren?* I thought as I parried one of his limbs. The other tore a bloody gash along my thigh. Then I was under him, and eight metal stakes were rising and falling all around me, striking the cobbles with enough force to shatter them as Bosch did his best to impale me without being able to see me. It couldn't have lasted more than a half-dozen heartbeats, but for that brief eternity I was certain I was going to die as I twisted desperately to avoid being punctured.

And then there was an enormous *KRUMP* sound. Above me, Bosch's body crumpled inward as if a hundred war hammers had struck it all at once.

Bosch staggered drunkenly away, the weird lights that played upon his now twisted body dimming. When they died out, he fell, motionless, to the cobbles.

"Sorry I was late," said Holgren as he staggered up to me, clutching his side. "Bosch evidently expected me as well, and prepared a reception." I looked past him, down the street, and saw a wet lump about as big as a horse but covered in scales, ichor still spurting out of it in time to a slowly fading heartbeat.

"Better late than never."

CHAPTER 29

Both of us were tired and bleeding, and I had only a bare hour or so before I was supposed to give the toad to Heirus. But we couldn't just leave the hell-spawned mess that had been Bosch and his daemonette lying there on the street. I ripped my ruined jacket into strips to bind up the worst injuries while Holgren did some magely thing to get hold of Kluge involving a prism—apparently they'd exchanged some sort of magical calling card that let them contact each other.

Once I'd stopped my blood from watering the cobbles, I offered to do the same for Holgren, but he waved it away.

"I'm going to check on Locquewood," I said, and he nodded.

"I'll wait here, and keep an eye on these things."

I found and lit a lamp in the front of the shop, then carried back to the storeroom.

He was dead. And mutilated. It was about as bad as I had expected. I hadn't known him well, but I don't think he would have wanted to survive what Bosch had done to him.

Most of him was sitting in a delicate chair behind a delicate desk. I made a mental note to ask Bollund if he'd had any family. If Bollund lived.

I was about to turn and go back out to Holgren when the package caught my eye.

About the size of my fist, it lay on the floor, half-smashed, obviously knocked there in the scuffle. It's beautiful wrapping was spattered with Locquewood's blood. I looked closer and saw my name written on the sky-blue paper it had been wrapped in. It looked like a feminine hand, one not terribly accustomed to writing.

I picked it up, heard the tinkling of broken glass from inside it. Carried it and the lantern back out to the street.

Holgren was bent over Bosch's remains, trying to wrench off the amber block that held Bosch's head.

"Souvenir?" I asked him.

"Ha. I want to retrieve it before Kluge arrives, which should be quite soon. Gavon will demand proof if you want the contract cancelled and your money back. Or had you forgotten?"

"Actually, I had." Hopefully Heirus had cancelled the contract, but a little insurance was welcome.

With an audible crack the head came free. "There, that's got it." He turned to hand it to me, saw my hands were full.

"What have you got there?"

"The answer to a mystery, maybe." I told him about Estra Haig's girl looking for me, leaving a package for me with Locquewood.

"Why Locquewood?"

"I don't know. Maybe the answer's inside."

"So why aren't you opening it?"

"I don't know. I've just suddenly got a strange feeling I won't like whatever it is."

He just looked at me.

"Alright, alright." I put the lamp down and tore open the wrapping, exposing a square little rosewood jewellery box, sadly splintered in one corner. I lifted the latch.

Inside was a scented piece of paper, folded small to fit, and bits of colored, broken glass. Broken glass I recognized from part of one green wing and from the delicate head and long, thin beak.

The hummingbird that Corbin had swiped from me the day before he died.

I fished out the note and set the box down. Unfolded the stiff, scented paper:

Madam Amra,

Corbin told me the bird had come from you, so I return it, and to show what I next write is the truth.

Corbin was my man. Madam Estra holds my indenture, and he was going to pay it, to buy it out so he and I could be together. But Madam Estra didn't like it, hated it in fact, that Corbin had chosen me to love.

I know Corbin is dead and gone. I knew it as soon as you came into the Dream to tell Madam Estra. His name on your lips and the look on your face told me all. But you didn't know about him and me. And I couldn't tell you, not there under her roof. So I want to tell you that if Corbin came to a bad end as my heart tells me he did, it was Estra Haig that did the deed, or had it done rather, because that last night before Corbin never came back to me, she told me he never would. She told me I was hers, her property, and I could no more take her man than her hairbrush could, or her dog. And when I told her that was for Corbin to say, she laughed and told me Corbin wouldn't be saying anything anymore.

Corbin told me you were a fierce one, and that if I was to find myself in trouble, you was the one to find if I couldn't find him. I'm not asking for anything, except for Corbin. If you're looking for the one who laid him low, then now you know.

I leave this with Corbin's 'connection' as he never told me where to find you.

Sincerely,

Lyra Juvis Blackdaughter

"That bitch." I hissed.

"Which bitch would that be?" Holgren asked, but I only half-heard him.

"She sat there, twisting her napkin in despair, offering me assistance in hunting down Corbin's killer, the fucking *picture* of sorrow!" I kicked the jewellery box down the street, scattering bits of colored glass along the cobbles.

Holgren carefully took the note from me. Read it. Handed it back. I crumpled it in my fist, then forced myself to calm. I smoothed out the letter, folded it back up carefully and stuck it in my pocket.

"So you're going to kill her?" he asked.

"Me? I'm a law-abiding citizen, Holgren. Especially when there's an inspector in the vicinity." I pointed my chin down the street, where a carriage had just turned the corner, with a dozen city watch trotting behind, armed with pikes.

"There's late, and then there's too late," I muttered.

Kluge didn't have anything to say to me, which suited me fine. He listened to Holgren's statement, then made a brief inspection of the shop and the corpses.

"Where's this one's head?" he asked when he got to Bosch.

Holgren looked like he wanted to feign ignorance, but he pulled his cloak back and showed the grisly trophy.

"Is there a particular reason you want that?" Kluge asked him.

"Yes."

"Do I want to know what that reason is?"

"Not really, Inspector."

Kluge let out a sort of disgusted sigh and said, "Get out of my sight, both of you." Then he gave his men some instruction regarding Bosch's corpse. They got busy wrapping the thing in a canvas tarp while Kluge set about burning the demon corpses with magefire.

"You heard the Inspector," I said to Holgren.

The sky was beginning to pink with dawn as we hobbled away towards my meeting with Red Hand.

CHAPTER 30

"I suppose you're coming with me, then?" I asked Holgren as we made our way towards the Necropolis.

"Well, it *is* on the way home," he replied. He was smiling, but his hand was pressed against the wound in his side.

"Got any magic for healing?" I asked. My back was still on fire, and the gash in my thigh wasn't much better. Both were going to severely restrict my mobility in a fight.

"Not my specialty, I'm afraid."

"Any idea what to do about Heirus?"

"Well, you have two options, it seems. Give him the toad. Or make him take it."

"I just wish I knew what he wanted it for," I muttered.

Holgren gave a short chuckle. "What would the king of assassins want with a god-forged weapon, I wonder?'

"That's just it," I replied. "I hate to say this again, but you didn't *see* him. I did. He doesn't need any magic blade to be the deadliest thing on two legs. It's not going to make him a better killer, Holgren. You can't improve on perfection."

"He obviously made an impression on you."

I shrugged, and darted out to hail a hack that had just turned the corner. At least I wouldn't have to walk the entire way to my doom.

~ ~ ~

The gates were open when we got there.

"Why don't you go on home?" I asked Holgren as we walked in.

"I think I'll stay with you."

"There's no point sticking your neck out. This isn't your fight, never was."

"So you've decided to fight?" he replied, avoiding my point.

"It's just an expression." We got to the hill, started climbing towards the Weeping Mother statue. It really was quite homely.

"I think I know you well enough now to say that you're wrong. It's become fairly plain that you, Amra Thetys, given the choice between fighting and capitulating, will pick a fight every damned time."

"You're saying I'm stubborn."

"Oh, yes, very much so. Contrary as well."

"No I'm not."

"Don't look now, but you're being stubborn. And contrary."

"I know you are, but what am I?"

That got a laugh out of him. But it died away quickly and his eyes got hard. I followed his gaze.

Heirus was standing directly beneath the Weeping Mother. He looked bored, and impatient.

As we closed to the last few yards, he spoke.

"You have it. Give it to me." He held out a hand.

"I have it," I replied. "But I need to know what you're going to do with it."

He cocked his head, and a confused look flitted across his face. "You know I can and will kill you, yet you continue to behave as though your needs, your *questions* matter."

"The question itself matters, not who it belongs to."

"Why?"

"Because I know you don't need this Blade to become more powerful. You are the deadliest man alive. So, Heirus, Red Hand, what do you intend to *do* with it?"

"An excellent question," said the Arhat, who had suddenly appeared a few yards away.

"I told you to keep that one away from me," hissed Heirus.

"And I told you he's not my dog," I replied.

The Arhat approached. "So, Kingmaker, Godslayer, why not answer the question? You well know what will happen if the Blade is loosed. What do you want with it?"

"What I want with the Blade is none of your concern."

"You know that is untrue. I am tasked with guarding it."

"And you have failed."

"Not yet."

Heirus moved, and suddenly the Arhat had a knife in his gut.

"Now you have failed," sneered Heirus into his face. That's when Holgren broke the magical chain around my neck.

"Remember," he whispered as it fell to the ground, "don't kill yourself." Then it hit the grass and everything changed.

With a thought, the world stood still. I looked around me, and it was like looking at a painting. Holgren stood, lips still shaped around the last sound he'd uttered. The Arhat stared into Heirus's eyes, his face only just beginning to show the agony of steel in his intestines.

I made two knives appear and began to walk towards them. "Come on then, Red Hand," I said and his head whipped around to me. "Let's see how good you really are."

He smiled and pulled his knife out of the Arhat. He actually saluted me with it. And then he flew at me, *still* a blur.

With a thought, I forced Holgren's magic to match him, and met his thrust from a half-decent guard position, knocking his knife hand away to my left with my wrist and following it with a thrust of my own with the knife in my right hand. But he had already spun away.

"You cannot sustain such magic. Either the toll it takes will kill you or I will. You cannot win."

I returned to the *Aquila* guard position, sideways to him, left arm and leg extended and right arm above my head, circling slowly, ready to strike from on high. It had been a long, long time since I'd been in anything like a formal knife duel. But you never forget. He was right, though; I could already feel the thirst building, as if I'd had nothing to drink for a long, hot day. He could just toy with me until I collapsed.

So I attacked.

I pushed the magic even harder, and came in with a showy feint to his eyes with my right while I drove my left down toward his groin. He jumped back, and back again, and gave me a shallow slice across the back of my left hand for my trouble.

"I could have had your thumb," he said, and I knew he was right.

I was good with a blade. He was much, much better.

When the cramps started I couldn't think what they were for a moment. Then I realized they were hunger pangs; hours, days perhaps of hunger compressed into an instant. I gritted my teeth against them, and the aching flesh of my back, and the ragged gash across my thigh, and pushed the magic once more, and flung my right-hand blade. I was hoping—praying, really—that once it left my hand it would not suddenly slow.

It didn't.

It took him in the throat. He hadn't even tried to block it.

His eyes got wide. His mouth sagged. He made choking sounds.

And then he pulled my knife out of his neck and laughed at me.

There was no hole in his neck. There wasn't even any blood.

I sat down on the grass and put my head in my hands.

"Can I have my toad *now*?" he asked.

CHAPTER 31

"Kerf's balls." I looked up and he was just standing there, smiling at me. Behind him, to my right, the Arhat was still dying by inches, a crimson stain spreading ever so slowly across the saffron robes over his stomach. *Why didn't you change forms? It might have given you a chance.* But he wasn't ever going to answer that question now.

I glanced behind me to my left, and there was Holgren, hand still raised from breaking the chain, infinitesimally moving back to his side.

I let go of the magic. The Arhat fell to his knees, then rolled onto his side. He was dead, or so close as made no difference. No help could get to him in time. Foolish boy. What had he hoped to accomplish?

Holgren came to stand behind me, and I could feel his power. He'd summoned up some sort of magic, and it was making the little hairs on the back of my neck fairly twist and jump.

I dropped my forearms on my knees, considered the cut Heirus had made across the back of my hand, instead of taking my thumb. Beads of blood had formed along its length.

Blood.

"You want the toad?" I asked him. "There's still one more I think you'll have to go through."

"Who? The mage?"

I shook my head, and wiped the back of my bloodied hand across the emerald cemetery grass. "They say you should never, ever spill blood in the

Necropolis," I told him.

"Oh, really?" he replied. "And why is that?"

"Because the Guardian will notice. And investigate. And it's got a nasty disposition."

"Oh, I do," said a voice like a thousand tombs yawning open. "That I surely do."

It sounded as if the voice had come from above. I glanced up, and the Weeping Mother statue stared back down at me. She had changed.

There was no pity or compassion in that badly carved face now. It had been replaced with cruelty, and madness. A cold, cold wind started up, and the light bled out of the sky.

"Who shed blood here in this sanctified place?" she asked, "and whose blood was shed?"

"My blood," I replied. "His knife," I said, pointing at Heirus who, I have to say, wasn't looking all that bothered.

"I do not ask the *living*," she told me with contempt.

The tombs opened, and the dead poured forth.

I looked down the hill and saw Corbin walking towards me. Behind him were the three armsmen, and a whole host of the dead I neither knew nor cared to.

"Who shed blood?" asked the Guardian again, and half a hundred fingers, in various states of decomposition, pointed at Heirus.

"Whose blood was shed?" And the fingers moved to point at me.

"Don't forget him," I said, pointing to the Arhat.

"His blood has not yet fallen." The Guardian replied.

"Well that's splitting hairs."

"Rules are rules." She turned to face Heirus. "By what cause or right do you spill blood here?"

He sniffed. "An oath forsworn."

"What oath?"

"This one promised to bring me the statue she holds in her shirt, but refuses to give it up. Thus, is she forsworn."

That massive head swivelled back to me. "Is this true?"

"I said I'd bring it, not give it to him!"

"Now who is the splitter of hairs? Tut-tut." She shook her massive finger at me, then looked at the gathered dead. "Who here witnessed this oath?"

A dozen mouldering hands raised. Including, I noticed, Corbin's. He had come to stand beside me.

"Thanks a lot," I told him, and he shrugged.

"Here is my judgment," said the Guardian. "The woman, being known to the honest dead, and having her blood spilled where it should not be, may go free." Pause. "*After* she gives up what she agreed to, here on this sanctified ground."

Bloodied, near-mad with thirst, aching with hunger and my wounds, I swore in disgust and pulled the hated toad from inside my shirt. I threw it at Heirus's feet.

"Choke on it," I said.

He bent down to pick it up, and Corbin whispered in my ear, voice slurred a little by decomposition: "When the time comes, do not let her have the Blade. We are her jailers as much as she is our Guardian. *Keep the Blade from her grasp.*"

Heirus held the toad up before his face. "Finally," he said. Then he began to whisper words that stirred the hairs on the back of my neck.

"Kerf's crooked staff," I swore. "He's a *mage* too?"

As Heirus spoke, the golden toad began to melt. The gold ran down his arm like mud and pattered on the grass, not in the least hot.

"Oh, that's a nice trick," murmured Holgren, and then all at once it was free, and that sickening feeling I'd felt when I'd tried to sleep with it in my hiding place in the wall suddenly beat down on me, on everyone there, living and dead.

Heirus held it in his hand, a shimmering, writhing thing that seemed to take on a hundred forms with each heartbeat, shedding cold blue sparks and jags of light that died out a hand's breadth away from it.

He turned and smiled at me, gave me another mocking duellist's salute.

"You asked me what I planned to do with Abanon's Blade, thief. I will tell you. I will finally, finally exit this sorry world, and be free of it and all you mayflies. Farewell."

Then he plunged the knife into his own heart.

As he crumpled to the ground, Corbin pushed me forward, shouting "Now!" in that creaky, slurred dead man's voice. The Guardian was already reaching down to pluck the Blade from Heirus's corpse. I turned the push into a lunge.

My shaking, bloodied hand got there just before her giant stone one.

And Abanon began to whisper to me, driving for a time all sense from my mind.

CHAPTER 32

The next thing I can recall: I am stumbling, shambling. I do not trust my feet or my hands or my eyes. I do not trust my breath or the taste of my own sour spit. The Blade is talking, whispering, and it has terrible, terrible things to tell me. I try to drown it out "No. No no no no no," I say, but it doesn't listen to me.

I am not in the Necropolis. I do not remember leaving. But I remember the Guardian, furious, and Corbin telling me to go to the temple. I remember Holgren pounding the Guardian with his magics, distracting her so that I could escape. I do not remember what happened to either of them.

Just get to the temple. Bath's temple. Just get to the temple, that's what the small part of my mind is saying. The part that's not being drowned by the hate, an ocean of bile pouring into my soul.

This is what the Arhat dealt with since he was ten years old? I will light candles for him in the temple of the departed. I swear it. I swear it. If I survive.

The Blade was shifting, shifting, now no bigger than a needle, now as long as a spear. I had to hold tight, very tight as it writhed in my hand.

And the Goddess's Blade whispered to me all the way.

—*all these people on the street. Kill them. They deserve it and it would be so easy. Humanity, cockroaches all, deserving nothing more than being trod underfoot. What vile, foul sacks of meat, their breathing and grasping and fornicating and defecating. Shoving food into their faces, shoving their genitals at each other, shoving out more wailing, hairless monkeys at every turn who grow and grow and do more of the same. A blight. This city is a blight, a running sore on the face of the world. Scour it. These maggots deserve extinction—*

An unending monologue of hate. It was all in my own voice. And the worst of it was that most of me did not disagree. I knew I was nodding my head, even as my mouth moaned out its 'no no no.'

—fucking wagon, see how it's just been left there to block the street? Thoughtless, careless self-absorbed, self-centered apes all of them, just left to block the street and it's in the fucking way but it doesn't have to be—

The hand that holds the Blade twitches and the wagon just disintegrates into dust, along with the horse that was hitched to it. "NO no no no," I wail, and start to run.

What if a child darts out in front of me, or an old man blocks my way?

My natural impatience, magnified a thousand-fold, will be the death of—anyone. Everyone.

What if the sun shines too brightly in my eyes? What if I breathe a breath of less-than-fresh air? No. No no no. I can't carry this burden. I'm no Arhat. I cannot hold this Blade.

I run faster.

I hug the Blade tight, lest I lose hold of it accidentally again.

Soon Bath's temple appeared before me, and my 'no no no' gave way to relieved sobs.

~ ~ ~

Bath's acolyte was waiting for me on the steps of the temple. His look was serene.

"My Master cannot accept this burden," he said somehow through sewn lips.

"Oh, gods, please. I can't. I can't. I hate you. I hate him. I fucking hate him and I hate your fucking secrets you pile of stinking—" I slap my hand over my mouth.

—miserable shit never meant to help anyone or anything his only secret is the terrible things he does to worshippers in a dark back room while his god watches—

He leaned forward and put a hand on my shoulder. I hated him for it.

But then I hated him for everything.

"What do you imagine would happen if a god who knew all the secrets of the world, of creation itself, felt the hate that you feel right now? No, Amra; this burden cannot come to rest with Bath."

"Then where?" I choked out. "I can't. I can't—"

"No," he said gently. "You can't either. But Bath knows a secret that he wants me to share with you." And he leaned down and whispered in my ear.

He whispered for a long time, for all that it was a single word. The word was very long, and it was forged in the fires of creation. I say it was a word, because that's how Bath chose to express it to me, but really it was a single, pure, undiluted concept.

No, it was not love. Love is not the opposite of hate. In fact, they're closer than you might think.

What *is* the opposite of love, you ask? Or hate, for that matter? I have no clue. Bath didn't share that secret with me.

What Bath shared with me was the undiluted truth of Apathy, the rat-fucking bastard, and it worked.

And what is Apathy? Best I can describe it is fatalism mixed with utter indifference. Things are as they are. Things will be as they will be. No point thinking about them, much less worrying. No point doing much of anything at all, as a matter of fact.

The acolyte whispered that terrible Word into my ear, and I collapsed on the steps like a puppet with cut strings.

The Blade poured its poison into my ear, and I no longer cared. Not about that, and not about anything else, either. Left to my own devices, I would have lain there on the steps of the temple until I starved to death or died of thirst. I was a motiveless shell. My body breathed, my heart beat, but beyond that I did nothing, because I was indifferent to everything. A mote of dust drifted into my eye and it was meant to be so. Blinking was futile.

Bath had pulled the Blade's fangs. He'd also turned me into, essentially, a breathing corpse.

"My Master did bid you be careful of the Eightfold Goddess, Amra," he said as he grabbed me under the armpits and began to drag me up the steps. "Well. Bath is the lord of secrets. He keeps them well. He will keep you well as well. What is another secret to Bath?"

He was dragging me up to the inside of the temple where, presumably, I'd disappear for good. Just another secret kept. Every blade needs a sheath.

Hate and apathy. The unstoppable against the immovable, and me being ground down in between. We were almost at the top of the stairs.

"Secrets are power," the Acolyte whispered in my ear. "How does it feel to be powerless? Useless and used? A tool for powers far greater than you?"

I felt hate for him, then. No, I felt... not hate. Rage.

I felt rage. And beneath that, terror.

Against the lifeless nullity of apathy and the corrosive torrent of poison that was the Blade's hate, rage blossomed in me. It burned and it cut and slowly made its way to my mouth as a scream.

I am no one's tool.

The echoes of that awful Word he had poured into my ear burned away to nothing, to silence. The Blade's vile whispering stuttered, stopped. The acolyte stopped dragging me and whispered a final time in my ear.

"Some secrets cannot be shared. Some secrets must be discovered."

I lay there on the steps and gasped, trembling with rage. I felt I had to stay still, or I would burn the world down.

The Blade had stopped its ceaseless, restless shifting. It was a throwing knife now. Perfectly weighted for my hand. For the first time it addressed me directly.

I will be your tool. I was meant *to be your tool. Use me, Amra.*

"Shut up," I told it. And it did.

The rage inside me screamed, inchoate, on and on. If I gave into it I knew the world would burn. I knew it. I could not let it slip its leash. Slowly, with great care, I sat up on the steps and looked at the acolyte.

"I know a secret or two as well," I told him through clenched teeth. "Secrets have no power. Not by themselves. It's the *control* of secrets that's power. Control is power, isn't it—Bath?"

He nodded. "Some secrets cannot be imparted. They must be discovered."

"And if I had not discovered this secret? Would You have salted me away in some secret place, to absorb the Blade's hate forever?"

"Yes," he said, without the least hesitation.

"At least You're honest." I climbed to my feet and carefully started down the steps. I couldn't look at the god of secrets. The rage inside me wanted to reduce him to ashes. A rage that was wholly human, wholly mine.

"What will you do with the Blade?" he called after me.

I kept walking, but said over my shoulder, "I could tell You it's a secret, but really it's just none of Your fucking business."

His laughter followed me down the strangely deserted street.

CHAPTER 33

Another secret Bath surely knew, and kept to himself, was that control is an illusion.

I'd built myself a bridge of rage, but as I walked across it, it disintegrated behind me. I had broken free of the Apathy the god of secrets had laid on me. But with the removal of the threat of being secreted away in some corner of his temple for eternity, a breathing corpse, a receptacle for the Blade's hate — with that threat avoided, it was hard to keep hold of my wrath.

The Blade was quiescent, but I didn't trust it. The old priest of Lagna was right; it *wanted* to be used. And if I did use it? What then? How could I possibly trust it? How could I trust myself? I was riding a dragon. Whatever control I believed I had, there would be a reckoning as soon as I turned loose.

And if I never turned loose? If I used Abanon's Blade as it wanted me to? Heirus was right. I could use the Blade to do awful, magnificent things with just a shred of hate and the will to see it through.

Yes, Amra. Show me what you hate, and that we will obliterate.

"I told you to shut up."

Traitor's Gate had seen better days. Better centuries, maybe. The gate itself was long gone. The pale yellow stone was fissured, and the narrow steps leading up to the abandoned guard room above were choked with refuse. But the oak door to the guard room was still relatively sound, and the lock sturdy. I should know, since I installed it myself. Another one of my bolt-holes. One with a nice view of the market, and a stupendous reek of rotting produce.

I sat in the window, on the wide ledge, looking down on the afternoon bustle. By this time of day most of the greens were limp. People haggled. Children darted amongst the makeshift tables, playing and shrieking.

I held the Blade in my hand. I couldn't put it down.

What did I hate?

I thought on it for a while. Could I actually use the Blade for some sort of good?

"Blade, could I use you to, say, kill every rapist in Lucernis?"

It throbbed in my hand. *Yes. Yes. We will hunt them down and make them pay-"*

"No. I mean right now. Can you make every rapist just drop dead."

Its silence was all the answer I needed.

What did I hate?

"Blade, can you end hunger? Poverty? Deformity in children? Can you heal the sick? Can you do one useful fucking thing other than destroy?"

Silence.

"You're bloody useless, aren't you?"

I am the hate of a goddess made manifest. I am a Power.

"You know what I think? I think she discarded you because you were *useless.* No, more than useless. A hindrance. A liability."

I could extinguish the sun. I could rip the world in twain. I could drown nations in rivers of blood. The stones of the gate tower trembled.

"But you can't fill one child's empty belly, or cure a cough, or even get a stain out of linen."

Tools are made for a purpose. They have a function, sometimes many functions. Their existence is *predicated* on their usefulness.

A tool that cannot be reliably taken in hand, fit for no useful purpose: Was it even a tool, in any rational sense of the word?

This Blade I held wasn't broken; it was flawed from its very creation.

It must have sensed the direction my thoughts were leading, because it began to vibrate in my hand, its form flickering from one type of cutlery to another. A dull keening started up from it, and a hellish red glow.

"A workman relies on his tool to do the job at hand. His skill, his hand, guides the tool. A tool that turns in his hand should be discarded."

Yes. Discard me. Leave me here—

"But no responsible craftsman would leave a dangerous tool lying around for any fool to pick up. Even swords, meant only for killing, come with scabbards."

Then find a sheath for me. I will lie quiet.

"Ah, but every tool, flawed or not, put away or left out, holds the potential to be used again." I held it up before me, looked long and hard at its coruscating form. Felt the hate bubble up like hot bile. Let it.

"You asked me what I hate. I'll tell you. I hate *you*, you useless—"

There was a soft *pop*, and a soft sigh. In my hand was only grit and ash, and tiny bits of charred bone.

I wiped the residue on my thigh, but it left a gray stain on the skin of my palm. I didn't think that stain would go away any time soon.

After a time, I got up and walked down the steps. I still had one more job to do.

I still had to tell Osskil who'd killed his brother.

With Abanon's Blade dust, I found I'd lost my thirst for revenge. After everything that had happened, dealing with Estra would just have been an unpleasant chore. But it might still mean something to Osskil.

CHAPTER 34

I t was a beautiful robe. No, beautiful did not do it justice. The robe was exquisite. Made of the finest silk, it lay in an almost liquid pool of itself, every ripple casting a lustrous crimson sheen. It probably cost what I made in an average year. It was probably the costliest bathing robe ever made. I reached to touch it, and he closed the lid of the carved, lacquered box.

"Better not," said Osskil. "Only the interior has been... treated. But why take a chance."

It was odd, having him here in my rooms. All I had for him to sit on was a decrepit sea chest. He didn't seem to mind.

I looked into his eyes, saw the flicker of some deep passion. Something hotter than rage. Something colder than revenge. Then he blinked, and shrugged, and the raw emotion subsided beneath the lordly demeanor.

"All the time we thought it was about some Goddess's artefact," he murmured, "when in fact my brother was murdered over the basest of human emotions. Jealousy."

I shook my head. "It's not so simple, I think. Estra Haig has been a great beauty all her life, and it's slipping away from her now as she grows older. When Corbin threw her over for a younger, prettier girl, it must have struck her at her core, her very sense of self." I rubbed absently at my hand, permanently marked by the Blade, or its residue. A barely visible discoloring of the skin; virtually unnoticeable compared to all the other scars I carry, and an itch that wouldn't go away. I'd learn to live with it. I've learned to live with much worse.

"Anyway, in a real sense it wasn't jealousy. It was desperate denial," I said.

After a short silence he said "Well, I suppose it doesn't matter, really. Betrayal is betrayal, and traitors always find compelling reasons to excuse their actions." His heavy-lidded gaze rested, unblinking and again hot, on the box.

"How long will it take?" I asked.

He shrugged. "Who can say? If she towels herself thoroughly first, perhaps fifty heartbeats before she notices anything. Much faster if she wears it wet. Either way, she will be a long while about the business of dying. The spasms will be ferocious. People poisoned thus have been known to break their own backs, the muscles convulse so furiously." His eyes may have shown emotion, but his voice displayed none.

I shuddered. "A terrible way to die."

"Poison is the prescribed death for traitors."

"Why?"

"Because traitors poison faith and trust."

"I mean why tell me about this at all?"

He was silent for a long time. I began to believe he would not answer. Then, "I loved my brother. My father sent me to see justice done because it was expected. But he despised Corbin. I'll never be sure why, but I think it was because Corbin favored Mother so much, in his looks. If only he'd looked a little less like her...."

He looked at me. "Because, of all those searching for my brother's murderer, only you did so not because you were ordered or paid to. Because you shamed me in that prison.

"Only you and I know the world grew a little darker at his death. Only you and I and this damned dog."

There was one other who probably knew, but I didn't bring up Corbin's lover. Best leave well enough alone, I thought.

Osskil reached down and scratched behind Bone's ears. Holgren had brought him round the day before, saying he was going somewhere for a couple of days, and that I needed a guard dog more than he did. When Osskil had first seen Bone, and been told it was Corbin's dog, he'd immediately asked if he could keep him. I couldn't say no.

"You were in on the beginning of it all," he said, pulling me back from my thoughts. "It is only fitting you know how it ends."

"Speaking of the dog," I said, changing the subject, "are you sure you want to burden yourself with such an ugly mongrel?" I hated to admit it, but I was going to miss Bone, slobber and all.

"Mongrel? This dog is a pureblood royal boarhound. He has the best lines I've ever seen of the breed. It would not be uncommon for one such as Bone to fetch more than a warhorse would. How he ended up on the streets of Lucernis, I'll never fathom."

"You're joking."

"My family breeds the finest dogs in Lucernia. I never joke about dogs."

I could think of nothing to say. We sat there for a while in silence, a thief, a baron and a royal cur. Then he rose, a beautiful, horrible death tucked under one arm.

"Thank you for the wine. If you are in Courune, and not then spectacularly at odds with the law, I would consider it an honor if you would call upon me." A ghost of a smile touched his heavy lips.

"You'll make a practice of taking in strays if you aren't careful. But all right. If I am in Courune, and not employed, I'll do just that." A thought occurred to me. "When will you send it?" I pointed at the box under his arm.

"I will call on Madame Haig personally this afternoon. We will pass pleasantries. I'll make discreet noises to the effect that she should not consider trying, in any fashion, to leverage her relationship with Corbin to gain anything from the Thracens. I will give her this gift as a token of my admiration. I wager she will think it no more than her due. And she will be right."

"What about whatever thugs she hired to kill Corbin? Will you hunt them down as well?"

He shook his head. "I don't see much point in that," he said. Silently, I agreed.

He left then and, shooing Bone before him, stepped into the gilded carriage waiting outside my door, oblivious to the threadbare crowd that had gathered to gawp at such a sight, in such a neighbourhood.

~ ~ ~

A couple of days later I found myself in Loathewater, one of the many slums of Lucernis. The day had dawned grey and heavy with rain that refused to fall. I hadn't been able to sleep much or well, what with all the punishment my body had taken over the past few days, and so I found myself doing what I always seem to do when at loose ends; walking aimlessly, trying to keep ahead of my thoughts. Or trying at least to tread water, so to speak.

I'd set out to kill Corbin's killer. I might not have done it with my own knife, but it was done. Estra Haig was a dead woman, whether she knew it yet or not. Along the way a lot of others had gotten dead. Some had deserved it. One, at least, had desired it. But I couldn't help but wonder if things wouldn't have been better off, in the grand scheme of things, if I'd just let well enough alone.

After all, none of it had brought Corbin back.

I'd walked most of the night away and on into the dawn when I looked around and found myself surrounded by the scrap shanties and towering trees of Loathewater. The sudden feeling of being watched had pulled me out of my ruminations.

She was standing in her doorway. She, like her house, was crisp and clean and straight, though the neighborhood was dilapidated, quietly desperate, and muck-strewn.

The bloodwitch.

"Seems you've found your way to my door," she said.

"Just passing through."

"Oh, come now. I knew you'd be around. I Saw it. Come inside then, and have some tea."

"No offense, but I'd rather not."

She smiled. "We each of us do things we'd rather not. It's part of life. There are things we should discuss that are best not spoken of on the street."

I really didn't want to offend a bloodwitch. Still, I hesitated.

"Come, I'll feed you as well. You look like the type who enjoys a scone."

My stomach rumbled. I went inside.

The interior was sparse and almost harshly clean. I don't know what I expected. Jars of newt eyes and bats in the rafters, maybe. Instead it reminded me of how my mother had kept her house, all those years ago. I could almost hear her muttering "poor's no excuse for filthy" the way she had when she was scrubbing something.

There was tea, with honey, and freshly toasted scones, with raisins, all on a little table set for two. I'm not all that fond of raisins, but the scones did smell good.

"You Saw me coming? Or do you lay out breakfast like this every day?"

"I know why you don't like me, Amra Thetys," she replied. Or didn't reply.

"How can I dislike you? I don't even know you."

"But you know what I am, and what I can do. You hate the very idea of fate, and so how could you be comfortable in the presence of someone who can See it?"

I took a sip of tea while I considered what she'd said. It was true, as far as it went.

"I don't doubt you have the Sight. But I'd make a distinction between seeing the future, however cloudily, and knowing what fate has in store for someone. If fate even exists."

"Oh, it does, though I won't bother trying to convince you of the fact. But you are right in believing seeing the future isn't the same as knowing what fate has in store."

"I wouldn't have expected you to agree."

She shrugged her thin shoulders. "To see the future is to see the likeliest route of a journey. To know fate, my dear, is to know the destination. I Saw your future, dear, and I'm sorry to say that it is a dark and bloody one, for the most part."

"Was. That's over. Abanon's Blade is no more, and Red Hand is dead. I'm done with your Eightfold Bitch."

She smiled, and while there was a little pity in it, it seemed to me there was far more of something I'd call contempt. But then I generally assume the worst of people unless given a reason not to.

"I've Seen your future, and something of your fate. While you think you are done with the Eightfold Goddess, She is far from done with you. You will have truck with gods and goddesses, demigods and demons, and Powers of the Earth and Aether before you breathe your last—"

I stood up, knocking back my chair. "Why the hells would you tell me such things?"

"Because they are true."

"So *what*? What good does it do me?"

"Because you need to prepare."

"And just how the hells do you suggest I go about doing that?"

She looked down at her scone. "I don't know. That's for you to discover."

A hot flash of anger surged through me. "And there, *right there*, is why I want nothing to do with Seers. Because for all your signs and portents, however true they might be, you never offer a scrap of useful advice, and you never, *ever* offer the simplest shred of hope. Fate is a slaver, bloodwitch, and I refuse its chains."

As I walked out her door, she spoke in a quiet voice.

"That is why fate has singled you out, Amra Thetys."

~ ~ ~

Holgren found me at sunset. I was sitting on the breaker wall just north of the harbour, staring out at the darkening sea, not thinking much of anything, if I'm being honest.

"The sunset is in the other direction," he said, sidling up beside me and leaning on the rough stone.

I grunted. "I've seen enough sunsets in my life. How did you find me?"

"The ways of the magi are mysterious," he said with a small smile. He held out two pinched fingers. It took me a moment to see the hair trapped between them.

"You left this on your first visit to my sanctum."

I gave him a flat stare. "That's a bit creepy."

He shrugged and let the hair float down to the restless sea below us. "Speaking of hair, yours is coming in quite nicely."

I had nothing to say to that, so I didn't. The silence stretched, but it wasn't uncomfortable.

"I've got some bad news," he finally said. "Gavon is gone."

"What do you mean, gone?"

"Gone, disappeared, vanished."

"With my money. Of course."

"I'm afraid so. But Daruvner said he'd like to see us once we've recuperated. There's a commission he thinks would be perfect for us."

"Are you broke, too?"

"Not really. But I may have mentioned that I was open to commissions if you were involved."

"What? Why?"

He smiled and raised an eyebrow. "I told you before. You're capable, and you have two wits to rub together. And you do get up to the most interesting goings-on." He put out a hand. "Partners?"

I looked at him. I realized for the first time that I trusted him without question, for all that he was a mage. Realized, however much I didn't want to, that in the past few days I had come to rely on him. Realized with something close to shock that I was fine with that reliance.

And so I took his hand, and shook.

EPILOGUE

An age was ending. In the grand scheme of things, this was not such an uncommon occurrence. The Age of the Gods had been on the downhill slope for more than a millennium in any case. Soon magic would run dry, barring some unlooked-for intervention. Soon the gods and demons, those who still survived after the Wars and the Cataclysm, would take their longstanding squabbles on to some new plane of existence.

As for what would come next, well. Perhaps the Age of Humanity, of Invention, of Ingenuity. Or perhaps something entirely other.

In the Lower Realms and in the Upper, change was coming, and sentinels who had stood watch for thousands upon thousands of years were abandoning their posts, drawn to the siren call of re-creation, of rebirth, of a resetting of the cosmic board.

Soon there would be no one left to watch for the return of the Eightfold Goddess. Soon there would be no one left who knew what to watch for, or why. The signs and portents would come about, and none would be the wiser.

The first already had.

Abanon's Blade was dust, destroyed by a mortal's will.

The first of the eight seals had finally, finally been broken.

In Her hiding place, in Her self-made prison between the planes, She laughed, and stretched Her fearsome frame.

AMRA'S WORLD

or, A Very Brief Guide To The
Known World, Inhabited By
Countless Multitudes, Among
Them Being One Particular
Thief Known As Amra Thetys

by Lhiewyn,

Sage of Lucernis, High Priest of Lagna the God of Knowledge
(Deceased),
Very Old Man

(Translated and edited by Michael McClung)

DEDICATIONS

Lhiewyn:

For Jessep, because everyone else I know well enough is dead. And stop "meditating" in the stacks, boy. I know what you're doing, and it will make you go blind.

Michael:

For all the readers over the years who have discovered Amra's world and come to love it as I do. Thank you.

THE WORLD: AN INCREDIBLY BRIEF OVERVIEW

The world is a big place. Really, really big. As far as we can tell, it is spherical, and it circles the sun, which is likely a big ball of fire hanging in the void. No, I don't know what it's hanging from. Don't be cheeky.

The stars are likely other balls of fire, either much smaller or much further away. Most are fixed, some move. Nobody knows why, and if anybody says they do they're lying. Oh, and astrologers, like children, should be beaten often on general principles.

There, wasn't that easy? You're welcome.

Oh, all right. So there's more to the world. The gods alone know why you'd want to know; probably to set out on some idiotic adventure far from home. I feel obliged to tell you that adventures are, on the whole, stunningly bad ideas, best avoided at all costs. Having spent thirty years wandering the world, I should know. I didn't get this useless leg from staying home and milking cows. Though, to be fair, cows can be bastards as well.

I'll tell you what I know. I very much doubt it will do you any good, but at least you won't be able to say I didn't warn you.

THE KNOWN WORLD: A SLIGHTLY
LESS-BRIEF OVERVIEW & HISTORY

Virtually everyone who isn't a liar or a drunkard agrees the world boasts two large landmasses, or continents. There is some credible speculation that a third continent exists on the far side of the world, but no real proof. Those who have gone looking for it haven't come back. Now they certainly might have found some veritable paradise where they were treated like kings and queens, and sensibly gave up any interest in returning and letting the rest of plodding humanity know about it. Let's just say I'm not inclined to believe this is the case.

Of the two continents we are certain of, the northern one is home to virtually all of humanity, and stretches for thousands of leagues from east to west. Elamners call it "Sulamel" which means Landfall. No other culture calls it anything in particular as people are, by and large, ignorant twits.

The southern continent (named "Lubania" by the intrepid and very dead explorer Rafe Luban but universally known as "Deathland" to everyone else) is roughly half the size of Sulamel, and is longer than it is wide. Those who have explored some small portion of it and returned (yours truly) report that it is a barren place of rock and sand and ruined cities, hot as all the hells combined, and full to the brim with interestingly horrid ways to die. If you take only one piece of advice from this old scribe, let it be this: Don't go there. Just don't.

If you do go, please have this tombstone made up beforehand:

I Went To Deathland Even Though
Lhiewyn Of Lucernis Told Me Not To
And Now I'm Dead, Because I'm Stupid

And no, I'm not going to publish my maps and notes from that expedition, because I don't believe in encouraging stupidity. So stop asking.

Right then. As for Sulamel, read on. Anyplace that is especially deadly, I'll (thoughtfully) indicate by writing in big, bold letters: "**Stay the Hells Away**." You're welcome.

But first, a bit of history.

I can hear you whining from here. "History is useless. History is boring. Tell me about the exciting and exotic lands," you're saying. Stop it. You're saying this because you're an idiot. History is important and you don't need all that much of it to keep you healthy. Those who do not learn from it are doomed to repeat it, and even worse, the rest of us will probably suffer the consequences. So pay attention.

Prehistory

Nobody knows where humans come from. The furthest back we can trace our mutton-headed race is about five thousand years ago. We probably came from the southern continent after we mucked it up good and proper. After all, somebody lived in those shattered cities, and unless you count grohl, we're the only animal that makes human-sized dwellings.

The Age of Legend

It's said that, thousands of years ago, the gods walked the World and interacted with humans on a daily basis. It was, according to some accounts, a golden age of peace, an idyllic epoch. This is bullshit. The gods warred against each other and used humans as their pawns. They killed us and each other in many interesting and horrid ways. I'm the high priest of a dead god. He didn't cut himself shaving.

This went on for an unknown but very long time. War after war, Gods killing gods, demons killing gods, gods killing demons, demons killing demons and everybody killing humans until, very roughly, some twelve hundred years ago. The final War of the Gods was fought to a standstill. Those divine and infernal beings still alive agreed to an armistice and signed an accord. They marked out their metaphysical territories, so to speak, and all the powers more or less stuck to tending to their knitting after that.

For two centuries, near enough, humanity had a bit of breathing room. Civilization, highly advanced in some areas and unheard of in others, took off like a cur with its tail on fire. Huge leaps were made in every area of human endeavor, from the magical Art to the mundane sciences. Some of it was due to the fact that cities weren't in danger of being leveled as collateral damage in one divine skirmish or another. Some more of it was due to the fact that those gods whose aspects aligned with human endeavor began to do their jobs consistently.

It was a good couple of centuries for mortals. Then, of course, we fucked everything up.

The Cataclysm

There was a group of very clever, very wise men (why is it always men?) who called themselves Philosophers. Some considered them mystics, others thought them deluded fools, but their Philosophy afforded them undeniably real power. It is said they could disappear in one place and reappear instantly in another. It is said they were almost impossible to kill. They weren't mages; in fact they looked down on the Art as a false trail to what they called "liberation." Liberation from what? I'm not getting into that. Somebody might think it a good idea and revive the whole mad shambles.

So. The Philosophers, in pursuit of their "liberation," decided that reality itself needed to be adjusted, so that it better suited them. They started adjusting.

Think of it like this: You're sitting on a stool. You're not satisfied with your stool. Maybe it's too low. Maybe you want to rearrange the legs. So, *still sitting on your gods-damned stool*, you start hacking the legs off of it.

If the Philosophers had had some *other* reality to shift the world to while they made their "adjustments" then perhaps it might not have been so rats-in-a-bag insane. Alas, we have just the one.

Evidence suggests they did their tinkering on an island off the southwest coast of Sulamel (**Stay the Hells Away**), if you trace backwards the spread of the Cataclysm.

But what exactly was the Cataclysm? Put short, it was a loosening of the natural order. One witness's account should suffice to explain:

> "The Cataclysm raced across the land, an unstoppable tide of unreason, first sickening and then severing every bond of nature and logic. Up became down, light became dark, the blood in your veins might turn to water or wine or molten lead. The very air might become poisonous vapor, or simply disappear, leaving countless thousands to suffocate like fish on land. You could not trust your senses. Silk could suddenly cut skin like razors. Between one moment and the next, your eyes might see something a thousand leagues or a thousand years removed. Reality itself was collapsing. Most living things died. Some became monsters. A few became dark powers, not far removed from gods."

The Cataclysm emptied virtually the entire western portion of Sulamel. Those who fled before it mostly ended up settling around the Dragonsea, eventually giving rise to the cultures and countries we are familiar with today. This mass exodus came to be called the Diaspora.

As for those lands humanity fled: There have been several expeditions over the last hundred years or so into what most call the Empty Lands or the Silent Lands (**Stay the Hells Away**). No human civilization remains. No humans remain. Those pinnacles of civilization that still live on in legend and imagination, such as Thagoth, Hluria, and Trevell, are either gone without trace or are shattered ruins.

There has been one organized attempt to resettle the Silent Lands. Two centuries and more ago a Lucernan prince hacked out a portion of the wilderness and founded a colony. He named it Haspur. For more than a decade Haspur thrived, trading in natural resources and taming the countryside around it.

Then, overnight, every soul in Haspur disappeared. No one has the least clue what happened to them.

On those maps that bother to mark it at all, the notation reads "Ruined Haspur" (**Stay the Hells Away**).

You'd have to be mad, desperate, banished or hunted to call the Silent Lands home.

The Diaspora

The Diaspora is a nice, neat name for a very messy period in history. What records there are, are generally fragmented. We know when it started, of course–the moment the Philosophers touched off the Cataclysm. But it's not as if everybody who was alive at the time just got up and headed out the door. Individuals, families, small groups, and entire nations fled at vastly different times, in every direction that was away from the danger that was engulfing the land in an unpredictable tide of chaos.

Survivors of the Cataclysm that fled eastward found accommodating lands to settle around the Dragonsea. They came in successive and overlapping waves, and by and large their strength at arms, technology and magic was far superior to the indigenous inhabitants. Those original peoples either assimilated, got pushed out, or expired. That's unpleasant, but then the truth usually is.

None of the old, pre-Cataclysm cultures survived unchanged either. Some morphed and became entirely new social constructs. Others blended and melded together, becoming hybrid cultures. A few kept the outward forms and observances that were their heritage, more or less. Generally less. Often you'll find they don't really understand the meanings or reasons for some of the more startlingly odd things they do, and if you ask them, they'll say that that's the way it's always been done. The real reason—obviously—is that people, by and large, are thought-challenged sheep.

Post-Diaspora

Right then. We've almost caught up to the present day, give or take eight centuries. If you want to delve into the minutiae of the history of every country on the Dragonsea, you've come to the wrong place. This person killed that person and became king. This country fought that country and won, then it fought another country and lost.... When you're my age, it all starts to sound like "blah blah blah people are bloodthirsty gits who never learn." If you really want to know more, say, about the Camlach occupation of the Low Countries, or the Helstrum-Elam wars, there are many thick, incredibly detailed, dusty volumes in the stacks of Lagna's temple in Lucernis. Just remember to drop a mark in the offering box. Silver is good, gold is better. And by all the dead gods, we do *not* lend out any materials. If you want a copy of something, you pay for Jessep to copy it out for you. And don't even think about trying to steal anything.

The Current Age

It's a little-known, rarely discussed, but undeniably true fact that the world is changing. The gods, rarely seen for centuries, seem to have disappeared entirely. Magic, the force that much of civilization once depended on, is increasingly being eschewed in favor of more mundane solutions to problems ranging from keeping rats out of the grain stores to killing lots of people quickly on the battlefield. Times are changing, even if people generally aren't.

Don't get me wrong. There are still lots of ghastly, dangerous beings of a supernatural bent roaming the world who would be more than happy to eat your face. Far, far too many deadly artifacts still litter the world, relics from the distant past waiting for the chance to wreak havoc once again. It's just that, for example, cities are more likely to fall from cannonade rather than the Art.

Why the change? Damned if I know. But the gods rarely get involved anymore and magic, from all indications, is on the way out. What this means for the future, I've no idea. But being a realist, I'd offer the caution that whatever comes next, it's probably not going to be rainbows and warm hugs. Good thing I'm as old as dirt and likely won't have to deal with whatever fuckery comes next.

And with that I end my incredibly brief yet inestimably useful treatise on the World and its history. You're welcome.

Oh, all right, there's a bit more I could say about the gods and religions and such. No idea why you'd want to know, but if you do, turn the page. Or don't. It's all the same to me.

THE GODS, GODDESSES, AND INFERNAL POWERS. ALSO, MAGIC

There used to be so many divine and semi-divine beings running around loose you couldn't keep track of them, like cockroaches scattering in sudden light, if I'm honest. But over the millennia they did a damned fine job of thinning themselves out by making war on each other. They're just not the force that they once were. Sure, a few people still worship this or that god or goddess, but for the most part deities are only useful when you really need to let loose with some crude language. Religion, per se, isn't really a motivating force. There are exceptions, of course; adherents of the Keddy faith can be annoyingly dogmatic, and in Camlach, devotion to their Prophet of the Fields isn't just lip service. But on the whole, people lost a lot of faith in the gods when they did fuck-all, for the most part, to prevent or even moderate the effects of the Cataclysm. People *believe* in the gods, certainly, just as I believe in bedbugs. Belief doesn't automatically lead to worship.

So let's make this easy on everybody, shall we? I'll just jot down a few of those immortal beings who still have some hold on the popular imagination in one fashion or another and we can all call it a day.

Bath: God of secrets. Fate unknown. Common epithet being "tighter than Bath's arsehole."

Gorm: Peace-bringer. Got impaled for his trouble. Common epithet being "Gorm on a stick."

Isin: Goddess of love. Fate unknown. Common epithet being "Isin's (usually creamy) tits."

Kerf: Hero-maker. Fate unknown. Too many epithets to list, but balls, back, beard and staff are quite common.

Lagna: God of Knowledge. Got his head chopped off by a Low Duke of the eleven hells for knowing the solution to a supposedly impossible puzzle. Common epithet being "Lagna's reward."

Mour: Goddess of preservation. Destroyed in the Cataclysm, some say while preserving the city of Trevell. If so she did a rotten job, since Trevell is nowhere to be found. Younger sister of She who Casts Eight Shadows. No known epithets.

She Who Casts Eight Shadows: Just don't. You think you want to know, but that's because you're ignorant of the danger. Sometimes ignorance is a good thing, for example when you're eating meat from a street vendor. (Un)common epithet: "The Eightfold Bitch."

Vosto: God of fools and drunkards. Fate unknown. No common epithets; Vosto's one of the few gods that people still pray to with real devotion. Or desperation. Same difference.

As for the denizens of the lower planes, the less said the better. I'll just leave it at this: The gods and goddesses sometimes helped mortals, when it pleased or amused them to do so. The infernal powers treat mortals as food, which is what we are to them, when all is said and done. You might play with your food, but you certainly don't help it.

Other Miscellaneous Metaphysicalities

There are an unknown number of planes comprising reality. The one we inhabit is generally called the mortal plane. There is at least one and likely several planes that the gods inhabit(ed) and there are, as everyone generally knows, eleven lower planes, or hells.

The number of planes of existence could be infinite for all I know. I'm the high priest of the dead god of knowledge, but he's unavailable for questioning, being dead, and the office didn't come with any special pointy hat of omniscience.

Some gods have temples, some gods have worshipers. It doesn't seem to matter much to people whether the god is dead or not, or whether he or she answers prayers. Mostly it does no harm, I suppose. Keeps the disgruntled from rioting in the streets for the most part, and temples are good places to meet people and exchange recipes and the like. Or at least I've found them to be.

There is one kind of temple that holds no god as its patron. You can find it in most cities around the Dragonsea; the temple of the departed. The survivors of the Cataclysm needed a place to mourn all that was lost, and the temple of the departed was their answer. They're usually grim, gray places, staffed by volunteers. Generally speaking, they're one of the few religious houses that are respected. Even during times of extreme strife, they don't get violated. So if you find yourself in a city being invaded, my advice to you would be to head for one of those temples and don't come out until the smoke clears.

What else? Ah, yes. Souls. Yes, you have one. Yes, it can be destroyed. Yes, you can sell it if you're an idiot, and can find a buyer. No, I'm not going to tell you how to do that, because I'm extremely grumpy, not pathetically amoral.

Magic

And then there's magic. It comes, essentially, in three flavors. There's divine magic, which I know fuck-all about, not being a god. There's the Art, which mages employ. And then there's whatever unnatural or supernatural power bloodwitches, seers and necromancers call on to do what they do. First, let's discuss the Art.

A mage is a person, generally but not necessarily male, who is able to sense and tap into the magic that permeates the mundane world. He is a person able to use that power, generally called his well, to enforce his will upon reality and alter it. Maybe he turns a pink flower blue. Maybe he makes your head pop off and roll down the street. The only real limits to what a mage is capable of reside inside the mage himself, and boil down to three questions:

1. What change can he imagine with sufficient clarity to convince reality it should be as he wishes it?

2. How determined is he to effect that change? Put another way, is he himself utterly convinced that the change is unstoppable, inevitable, more real than the reality he wishes to replace?

3. How much power does he have to draw on, to transform that change from an imagining to an undisputed, objective fact?

If you think it's easy, give it a try. Even if you aren't a mage. Go pick a flower and try to convince yourself it's a color other than what your eyes tell you it is. Go on. This book will still be here when you return, head throbbing.

No two mages are alike, not in their will, their imagination, or the depth of their well. In a very real sense, each mage practices a completely different sort of magic from every other mage. And that, I suspect, is why they call it the Art rather than the Craft, or the Science.

As for bloodwitches, necromancers and seers, they seem to derive their uncanny powers from some source other than that which mages do. Or, if magic were a river, they dip their buckets in a different tributary. They seem to have much less control over their powers, especially seers. Necromancers tend to rely much more heavily on ritual, bric-a-brac and other external paraphernalia, though whether it's just for show is debatable.

Bloodwitches are generally but not exclusively female. Many are also necromancers and or seers, to a greater or lesser degree, but their primary power seems to involve the use and manipulation of blood, as their name would suggest. They might cleanse the poison from a dying man's blood. Or they might have put it there in the first place. They might be able to track down a missing child, say, were a drop of the child's blood kept for such an emergency (and it often is in the Low Countries). They also might make a man's blood boil in his body. Literally. Or dry it up in his veins. Or they might create a blood doll, a simulacrum of the person who had donated blood for the purpose.

There is some speculation that bloodwitches, seers and necromancers trace their lineage back to the original, indigenous people of the Dragonsea area, while those with magely power are the descendants of the people of the Diaspora. How much truth there is to such speculation, I honestly do not know, though I suspect there is something to the notion. But one thing is certain: none of them make good enemies.

I think that about covers the metaphysical aspects of the World. What, you want to know more? At the risk of repeating myself, if you want to know more, there are many dusty tomes, etc. Temples don't keep themselves from falling down, you know. They require donations and offerings. And at Lagna's temple, you get access to the knowledge of the ages in return, rather than some feel-good singalong. Top that.

Right then. I'm old and it's time for my nap. If you want to know more and you can't find your answer in the stacks, you're perfectly welcome to write to the paunchy, middle-aged scribe who's translating this, Michael Something-foreign-whatsit-lung, and he'll pass it along. If it's not an incredibly doltish question, I'll give you a reply. Eventually. If I don't die in my sleep between now and then.

-Lhiewyn

ABOUT THE AUTHOR

Michael McClung was born and raised in Texas, but now kicks around Southeast Asia. He has published eight novels, a novella and a short story collection. His first novel was published by Random House in 2003, and in 2016 he won Mark Lawrence's inaugural SPFBO contest with *The Thief Who Pulled on Trouble's Braids*. He goes by @mcclungmike on Twitter, but doesn't do the Facebook anymore, because reasons.

If you would like to receive word about Michael's writing-related stuff, why not **join the newsletter**? It is totally non-spammy. Just visit the following:

https://my.sendinblue.com/users/subscribe/js_id/2omax/id/1